THE MYSTERY OF SCHROON LAKE INN

THE CHRONICLE OF A LADY DETECTIVE

K.B. OWEN

CHAPTER 1

I took a breath as I tapped on the door to William Pinkerton's office. I hoped he would have a real detective assignment for me this time. Watching for shoplifters at Marshall Field's or fare skimmers aboard streetcars had paid a few bills, but was insufferably dull work. I had not hitherto been aware of a perverse streak in my nature that felt disappointment when people behaved themselves.

"Come in."

Every window was open in the corner office, but barely a paper stirred on the large mahogany desk. Chicago in summer can be hotter than Hades. I tucked away a damp strand of blonde hair that had yet again escaped my hat and tried to ignore the perspiration trickling beneath my shirtwaist.

Mr. Pinkerton, a burly man with a salt-and-pepper mustache and heavy brows, bowed politely. "Thank you for coming, Mrs. Wynch." He waved me into a chair.

I grimaced at the sound of my married name, although after

1

seven years of marriage—three of them living apart from Frank—
I should be used to it by now. "I would prefer you address me as
Miss Hamilton."

He gave a small shake of his head as he sat. "We've discussed
this before. There will, of course, be times when it's advisable that
you pose as an unmarried lady for the purposes of an assignment,
but here at the agency, we have always known you as Frank's
wife." He hesitated, his eyes softening. "Is there no chance of
reconciliation between you two?"

I clenched my gloved hands in my lap. "Absolutely none."

Pinkerton raised a disapproving eyebrow.

"I understood my work at this agency to be based upon *my*
merits," I retorted, "not the fact that Frank Wynch is on your
payroll."

"Of course, of course." His tone was one of soothing a fractious
child. "Your successful resolution of the Comstock matter leaves
no doubt as to your skills. I only wish we had more occasion to
put those talents to use."

I settled back in my chair. "I know you mean well. But you
must leave me to tend to my personal affairs."

He sighed. "As you wish." He passed over an envelope. "I have
an interesting assignment for you. The location is rather remote,
and I would prefer you not go alone. Your friend, Miss Leigh—
can we count upon her discretion?"

"Most assuredly, sir."

"Ah. Good, good. Would she be willing to accompany you?"

I hesitated. Until my Pinkerton assignments grew more regular, Cassie and I relied upon the meager income from our lodgers
along with giving lessons in piano and china painting. Perhaps we
could leave Sadie, our already-overworked maid, in charge for a
little while. "Accompany me where?" I hoped it wasn't a hotter
Southern locale.

His smile grew wide. "The Adirondacks."

I could feel my own smile matching his. The cool air of the

mountains was just what we needed. And to be paid for it—"I am sure I could convince her to come along."

"Excellent." He gestured to the envelope. "Inside are train, coach, and steamer tickets for the two of you. You'll be heading to the town of Bittern Point, where Schroon Lake Inn is located."

"What's at Schroon Lake Inn?"

"Until last year, only mice and rotting floorboards," he quipped. "A good friend of mine, Jacob Meyer, bought the inn and has been renovating it. In spite of a few setbacks early on during the renovation, he was able to open in time for the season. That was about two months ago. Things proceeded splendidly. A full house each week, the best clientele, favorable reviews. Until a couple of weeks ago."

"What happened then?"

"Ghosts."

The single word sent a tingle along my spine, even as my reason rebelled against such nonsense.

He shrugged at my skeptical look. "Meyer says several guests have reported strange noises in the middle of the night—footsteps on creaking boards, whispers, dragging chains, thumping sounds. Easily dismissed, until one female guest claimed to see the apparition of a man, coming through the wall of her bedroom. She screamed, and it vanished."

I suppressed a snort. "Sounds like the country lore that's told around those parts. Campfire stories."

"Except for the sighting," he pointed out.

"The woman could have been dreaming."

"Meyer doesn't think so," Pinkerton said. "He's convinced Atwater is behind it."

"Atwater?"

"Lionel Atwater, owner of nearby Cedar Lodge. He had the monopoly on the area's tourist lodging for a long time. He's been spreading the story far and wide that Schroon Lake Inn is haunted by the ghost of the former proprietor."

I frowned. "Who was the former proprietor of Schroon Lake Inn, and why would he haunt it now?"

Pinkerton fidgeted with a pen. "His name was Artie Willis. He built the place in the early sixties, ran it for more than ten years, then disappeared sometime in the winter of 1875. The local sheriff—well, not exactly *local*, the closest man is in Chestertown—investigated at the time, interviewed the staff and the man's associates. He and his volunteers scoured the inn and grounds. Some of Willis's clothes and other personal effects were gone. The staff said Willis's plan was to close up for the winter and leave the groundskeeper to see to the place. But Willis never returned. No body, no sign of trouble."

"If he's still alive, why would he simply walk away from the inn?"

Pinkerton pulled out a sheet and glanced down the page. "The property was heavily mortgaged...looks as if he was in danger of default. He may have taken what funds he had and made a fresh start." He shifted in his chair. "But I'm not sending you there to solve a ten-year-old disappearance. We have enough to worry about in the here and now."

I nodded. "Have the ghost story and accompanying shenanigans succeeded in putting off Mr. Meyer's guests?"

He smiled. "It's an ill wind that blows no good, Mrs. Wynch. Although several prospective guests who learned of the incidents *did* cancel their reservations, curiosity-seekers have been flocking to the inn."

I grinned. "I'm sure that vexed Atwater to no end."

"Probably. The ghostly incidents have continued, though reduced in frequency. Meyer believes Atwater has changed tactics to something far more devastating."

"Oh?"

"Last week, three guests had jewelry stolen during their stay."

I leaned forward. Now the case was getting interesting. "Valuable items?"

"Valuable enough. Meyer reimbursed them, generously, for the loss. He is insured, but the damage to the inn's reputation could be considerable. He has managed to keep it quiet. For now. He fired the most likely women responsible—two maids—though he has no proof. He also installed a brand-new safe in his office—" He broke off with a sigh. "I wish he had consulted me first before incurring such an expense."

I nodded. "No lady is going to keep her jewels in a safe." If it were a hotel in the heart of New York City, perhaps. But a lakeside resort in upstate New York? Mr. Meyer could not suggest such a measure without his clientele becoming wary.

"Indeed," he said. "And ladies are often careless of their baubles to begin with. A safe would do little good if the item were presumed stolen but was in fact misplaced."

Although I was inclined to agree with him, I did not appreciate the patronizing glance he sent my way.

"A thorough search was made for the items?" I asked.

He nodded.

"And he fired the maids, although he had no proof of their guilt?"

"He believes Atwater put the girls up to it. They do seasonal work for both establishments. Besides, the maids were the only ones besides the housekeeper who had keys to the rooms."

"Why not fire the housekeeper as well?" I asked.

"Housekeepers are more difficult to replace. And Meyer trusts Mrs. Davis implicitly. She has been working for him for years, moved out there with him to help run the place."

"Ah. Is there a *Mr.* Davis?"

"She has never been married, to my knowledge."

I nodded. Housekeepers often used *Mrs.* as a form of address. "Why ask for our help, if Meyer believes he has solved the problem?"

Pinkerton shifted in his chair. "There is still the matter of the ghost. He doesn't care to run an establishment that caters exclusively to thrill-mongers."

I suppressed a groan. I never thought I'd be in the ghost-hunting business.

"Meyer cannot afford to be sanguine about last week's jewel thefts, either," Pinkerton went on. "In four days, he is expecting a party of distinguished guests—the Barringtons—who could make or break the future of the inn. They arrive the day after you, with a number of their friends. It is a gold-plated guest list of influential people. You have heard of Miss Amalie Joubert, the opera singer, and Spencer Rayburn, the big game hunter? They will be there. If Meyer got it wrong and the maids were not responsible for last week's losses, he may still have a thief at the inn. I am counting upon you to prevent any further thefts during your time there. Should any member of the party suffer a loss, it would be disastrous for Meyer." He gestured to the envelope I held in my lap. "Names and details about the staff are in the report. Look it over later, and let me know if you have any questions before you leave town."

I frowned. "How am I to guard the baubles of so many without their knowledge?"

"That is for you to decide. But I can equip you with an excellent cover story, a persona to give you greater freedom during your stay." Pinkerton pressed the buzzer for his secretary.

I looked at him blankly.

The secretary opened the door. "Yes, sir?"

Pinkerton stood. "Show in Madame Violette."

I turned to see a slightly stout woman of forty carrying a well-worn carpetbag. Although her attire was an eclectic composite of fringes and ruffles, it was her heavily lashed, blue-violet eyes that demanded notice. She had lined them in kohl for emphasis. The effect was exotic and striking.

Pinkerton ushered her to a chair. "Welcome, Madame. So kind of you to join us."

The lady inclined her head. "As you have recently done me a service, sir, it is my pleasure." She examined me critically. "My, how tall you are! And your dress...no, no, that will not do at all. You look like a...schoolmarm."

I self-consciously smoothed my skirt. Schoolmarm, indeed. I admit, I am much too tall and angular for the current beauty standard, my eyes are light gray rather than heavily-lashed doe-brown, and most days I twist my blonde hair into an expedient topknot....

Well, perhaps there is a *bit* of the schoolmarm in me.

Madame Violette sighed as she exchanged a look with Pinkerton. "This one, she will need some work."

"To what end, pray?" I snapped.

Pinkerton sat down behind his desk again. "Why, to turn you into a spirit medium, of course."

CHAPTER 2

I looked from one to the other. "Surely, you are not serious."

Pinkerton rubbed his hands together. "I came up with the idea yesterday, after successfully resolving Madame Violette's little... problem. Since Meyer's hotel is purported to be haunted, would it not be natural for a spirit medium to wish to visit such a place? If she were of limited funds, she might contact the proprietor and offer to hold séances, card-readings, and so on for his guests, in exchange for free room and board for the week."

I closed my mouth when I realized it had been hanging open. Had it really come to this? I, Penelope Hamilton, whose family belonged to Boston's oldest social registry, masquerading as a hocus-pocus charlatan?

I sighed. I had willfully chosen this profession, for the sake of the adventure. Here was adventure, staring back at me.

Pinkerton went on. "Such an unconventional figure would be excused no end of eccentricities—begging your pardon, Madame," he added, with a quick glance in that lady's direction before turning back to me. "You may learn secrets that people do not even tell their father confessor and explore areas of the inn not typically available to proper ladies. I have asked Madame Violette to work with you over the next two days—your train leaves the day after tomorrow—to teach you the tricks of the trade."

I regarded Madame Violette as the woman sat primly, gloved hands in her lap. Could I learn enough of the medium's tricks in two days to fool everyone for a week?

William Pinkerton grew impatient with my silence. "Do you want the job or not, Mrs. Wynch?"

The spirit medium accompanied me on the bus ride home. Neither of us seemed in the mood for idle chatter, and as we could not discuss what was really on our minds in the company of strangers, we kept our thoughts to ourselves.

Uppermost in my mind was how I would explain this to Cassie. She would be delighted no end by a paid vacation at a mountain lake, but she was also superstitious. Séances and tales of ghosts walking at night might be sufficient for her to balk at such a trip. Add to that my bringing home Madame Violette to initiate me into her clan of charlatans and shysters? Cassie might run screaming down Oakley Avenue.

But she was my oldest and most loyal friend. We had practically grown up together, sharing many a girlhood secret. When I wrote to her three years ago about my separation from Frank, she had promptly left Boston and come to stay. She'd been with me ever since. Sometimes I worried that it was unfair to her. She had never married and was in no position to meet a suitable gentleman from the obscurity of a modest boarding house, living a hand-to-mouth existence that did not allow for new dresses and social entertainments. Still, she seemed happy, and I didn't know what I would do without her.

Cassie came down the front hall when we arrived, still wearing a flour-dusted apron.

"Madame, this is my friend, Cassie Leigh. Cassie, this is Madame Violette. She's helping me prepare for my new case."

Madame inclined her head and began pulling off her gloves. "A pleasure to make your acquaintance, Miss Leigh. What room will I be staying in?"

I gave her a sharp look. "*Staying in?*"

The woman nodded vigorously. "There is not enough time to travel back and forth. I live quite far from here, you see. And we have much work to do in the meantime."

She had a point.

Cassie's pursed lips and downward-slanted brows made obvious her displeasure. She turned to me, her look black as thunder. "May I speak with you?"

"Madame," I said, "why don't you wait in the parlor? It's cooler in there. I will join you shortly."

Once Madame had turned away, Cassie dragged me into the empty dining room before I had a chance to unpin my hat. She turned to me, hands on hips. "If that woman is staying the night, I'm locking up what little silver we have left. What has she to do with your new assignment?"

I grimaced. "It's a long story. But I have good news. We are going to the Adirondacks! Mr. Pinkerton asked that you accompany me. An inn by the lake, for a week, all expenses paid."

Her eyes widened with delight. "The mountains, for an entire week?" she breathed. "When do we leave?"

"The day after tomorrow. I have the train tickets. Can Sadie take care of things while we're away?"

Cassie grinned. "She doesn't visit her mother until the end of the month." She clasped her hands in excitement. "Oh, this is perfect!"

I sighed and inclined my head toward the parlor door. "Not quite *perfect*. The assignment requires that I masquerade as a spirit medium. Madame Violette is here to train me."

Cassie frowned. "A spirit medium?" She glanced uneasily at the parlor door. "There are some things that one should not meddle with, Pen. The afterlife is one of them."

I waved a dismissive hand. "It's all a charade. You know as well as I that there are no such things as ghosts. Trust me, I shan't be bringing spirit curses down upon our heads." I set aside my hat and smoothed my hair. "Madame and I had better get started. Can you and Sadie manage without me?"

She had already turned toward the kitchen, muttering all the while. "...may as well be gypsies in a sideshow. No good can come of this."

When I entered the parlor, I saw Madame was not alone. Mrs. Hobbs, one of our more flamboyant lodgers, with her fondness for advice columns, floral-print dresses, and expensive shoes two sizes too small for her flat feet, was sitting beside the spiritualist, drinking tea. Like attracts like, I suppose.

"Oh! Miss Hamilton, I have just made the acquaintance of your most interesting guest!" Mrs. Hobbs exclaimed. "What a shame she is not staying longer. I had hoped we could have a séance."

"But of course we can," Madame said. "The energies of this house are quite strong. I'm sure any number of people have died here."

Mrs. Hobbs nodded vigorously. "I have always felt that, too."

I snorted. "The house is only thirty years old. I doubt there is much calamity to be found."

Madame gave me a reproachful look. "This used to be Indian land. The spirits are strong here. Perhaps we can have a séance tomorrow?"

I shook my head. "*No séances.* I do not wish to become the laughingstock of the neighborhood." What sort of lodgers would we attract with such monkeyshines?

Madame did not argue the point but gestured to the nearly empty cup in Mrs. Hobbs's lap. "You wish me to read the leaves? We can do that, at least."

"Oh yes, please do!" The woman drained the last of her tea,

eyed the interior doubtfully, then passed over the cup. Madame waved me into the seat beside her. This was to be my first lesson.

She tipped the cup carefully toward the light. "Ah, yes, see this grouping here? It is a heart."

"Ooh, yes, I see it," Mrs. Hobbs breathed. "What does it mean?"

"Oh, it is good, very good," Madame reassured her. "It is a symbol of happiness coming your way, very soon. Either money or love."

Mrs. Hobbs clasped her hands to her bosom in delight. "Is there anything else?" She squinted into the cup. "They all look like muddled clumps to me. I should have brought my spectacles."

Indeed she should, as Mrs. Hobbs was quite near-sighted, but vanity kept her from wearing them. She was continually bumping into furniture. We had to remove every vase and knick-knack that once rested on the side tables.

Madame frowned in concentration. "Let us see…hmm, it looks to be a set of horns…." Her voice trailed off.

"That's bad, isn't it?" Mrs. Hobbs asked anxiously.

"I'm afraid so. Horns signify future betrayal. But…I could be mistaken. Let me take a closer look." Madame brought the cup over to the light of the window and examined further. "Wait, I see it better now. It is not horns, but a pair of hands."

"How extraordinary," Mrs. Hobbs said. "Is that good or bad?"

"Oh, it is quite good. A single hand is propitious of friendship and loyalty, perhaps even a bargain agreed upon or a beneficial meeting. Two hands together is a strong sign of a relationship." Madame looked at Mrs. Hobbs closely. "You are a widow, ma'am?"

The lady nodded.

"Has a gentleman recently shown an interest in you or been especially attentive?"

Mrs. Hobbs leaned forward eagerly. "Mr. Grissom, a fellow lodger, has been most kind to me lately."

I groaned inwardly. Poor Mr. Grissom. He would know no peace now, while Mrs. Hobbs harbored ideas of romance.

"Madame said that it may happen *soon*," I interjected, trying to spare the man. "Who knows? You may meet someone in the next few weeks."

"True," Madame said.

Mrs. Hobbs left shortly after that, no doubt to primp and preen in front of her looking glass in anticipation of Mr. Grissom's presence at dinner. I began stacking the tea things back on the tray and mopped up what had sloshed out of the cup. "Reading leaves is a messy endeavor."

Madame smiled. "But so easy to do. The eye sees what it wants to see. It is our nature to look for patterns out of the jumble. If you are convincing in your pronouncements, your clients will see the shapes you say and accept the meanings you indicate."

I nodded. "That time, when you were unsure about the shape you saw, was that part of a strategy?"

"It is good to create a little anxiety," Madame said placidly. "Then, when the news turns out to be good, the client is grateful and has taken the first step toward becoming dependent upon you."

I grimaced. "What a loathsome game you play."

"One must eat, Mrs. Wynch."

Hamilton, I corrected silently.

"It is harmless, really." She shrugged. "Come, sit. It is about to become your game as well, and we have much to do."

For the rest of the afternoon, I was immersed in the world of a spirit medium, becoming conversant with terms such as "the other side," "autonomous writing," "ectoplasm," and "spirit guide." I learned to manipulate the planchette, read cards in a tarot deck, swing a watch chain with no visible movement, and write upon a spirit slate.

I was not up to Madame Violette's standards with the spirit slate, however, which required me to wear a ring fitted with a small piece of chalk underneath and quickly write with it upon the slate while it rested in my lap under the table.

"No, no, no," she sighed, eyeing my latest attempt. "It looks like a chicken has tracked chalk dust across the board."

There was no denying she was right about that.

"We will have to leave spirit-writing out of your repertoire, but at least you have mastered the planchette and the cards. Let us move on to conducting a séance. How are you at voices?"

"Voices?"

"Can you imitate a man's voice? I understand that the ghost of the former proprietor of Schroon Lake Inn now haunts the establishment. Probably murdered," she added matter-of-factly.

I made a face. "How could I possibly know what Artie Willis's voice sounded like?"

"Unnecessary. It need only be masculine. In case your clients have doubts, you can remind them that when someone has passed to the other side and left behind their corporeal form, the voice often alters."

"Convenient."

Madame gave a small smile. "I have found it so. Now, let me hear you."

I affected a deep voice as best as I could.

"No, from *here*." Madame grabbed me around the waist. "More volume."

As I complied, Cassie had the misfortune to step into the room to announce supper. Startled, she grabbed a chair for support. "Mercy, you scared me to death!"

Madame gave a delighted laugh. "Most excellent, Mrs. Wynch. Hmm." She looked me over thoughtfully. "We must devise a more suitable name."

"What about Madame Strident?" Cassie said caustically. I chuckled, but Madame was all business.

"I am partial to using the name of a color. What about... Madame Cerise? It is a pretty name, and we can create a story of how you first saw a vision from the other world, bathed in a cerise-colored glow. We can work out the details later."

"Why not? Madame Cerise it is," I said. I had to admit I was beginning to enjoy myself.

"Good." Madame nodded. "After the meal, we'll go over what happens at a séance. Miss Leigh, we'll need your help then, too."

After the dishes were cleared and the dining room door closed to the rest of the lodgers, Madame Violette set to work. "Miss Leigh, you will be out of sight, listening for cues. That is when you will make the rapping noises. Mrs. Wynch—Madame Cerise—you will be sitting around the table with the guests. When you are ready for the session to end, you will cause the table to tip." She pulled out a thin, nearly invisible cable and several eyelet screws, motioning me to crouch down upon the floor. "Watch how I do this. I will give you the rigging to take with you to the inn, where you'll install it at a suitable table. It must be a light-weight one such as this, or it will not work."

I watched in fascination as Madame adeptly screwed in the device. A slight tug of the wire while in a seated position, and the table tipped, seemingly of its own accord. "Amazing."

"Now, you try." Madame motioned me into the chair.

It took me a number of attempts before I could tug the cord without drawing attention and without such force as to tip the table into my lap.

"Good, very good," Madame finally said.

The evening flew by as Madame walked us through the standard séance programme: the dimmed lights, the single candle, the bell beneath the glass dome, the circle of hands, the summoning of the medium's spirit guide, then the entreaty to the spirit in question to show himself. A few sharp raps and the ring of a bell. The medium succumbing to the spirit, who speaks through her. A few questions and answers, the violent tipping of the table to signify the spirit is displeased and is leaving, then the medium coming back to herself, supposedly unaware of what had taken place.

Madame showed me how to whisk the table wire out of sight should suspicion arise and coached Cassie on rapping and the props I might elect to use. I was gratified to see that Cassie's expression had transformed from wariness to avid participation. Perhaps seeing the tricks behind the scenes had dispelled her superstitious fears at last.

We practiced it all, over and over again. I wondered what my dreams were going to look like that night.

I need not have worried. When Madame finally released us to tumble into our beds, I was too exhausted to dream.

CHAPTER 3

*T*he next day started out with more practicing of the medium's tricks. Madame decided it was also time to work on my appearance. She cast a critical eye upon my current outfit, an eggshell pleated shirtwaist and serviceable skirt of amber linen.

"You do not look the part in such attire," she said. "Perhaps your boarder—the Widow Hobbs—could lend you something suitable? From what I have seen of her, such a wardrobe would be along the line of what you need."

I sighed. "I was afraid you would suggest that. Very well, I'll ask." Mrs. Hobbs was close to my height, but I would have to pin every waist, as the lady was over-fond of Sadie's stroganoff and possessed a hearty appetite.

Madame gestured toward my head. "And the hair...this will not do *at all*. Perhaps a turban?"

Land sakes, she was trying to turn me into a *swami*. I drew myself up to my full height, which meant I towered over the lady. "No. No *turbans*."

Madame Violette shrank back a little. "Very well. Let me see what I can do with your hair." She sat me down in front of a mirror and gathered up brushes, combs, scissors, and pins. I tried not to fidget as she experimented.

Cassie came in just as Madame had finished. She stopped in astonishment. "I must say, Pen, it looks much nicer than the tight topknot you usually wear."

She was right. Madame had pulled back my blonde hair more loosely along the sides and trimmed charming wisps in the front that softened the angular shape of my jaw. She had braided the length, arranging it in a coronet at the crown of my head.

"Thank you, Madame," I said. "I only hope I can duplicate this on my own."

"I'll help you," Cassie offered.

"You look quite regal," Madame said, stepping back to admire her handiwork. "Perhaps you were a princess in a former life?"

I rolled my eyes.

"Ah well, it will make an intriguing addition to your masquerade," Madame said with a shrug. "A colorful past—whether in this life or a previous one—is to be expected of us."

I felt the jolt of the word "us." I had graduated from Madame's tutorials. She and I were of a kind, for now.

Madame Violette left that afternoon. I took advantage of the lull just before tea time to knock upon Mrs. Hobbs's door.

The cheery woman raised her eyebrows in surprise. "Miss Hamilton! Please, come in." She opened the door wider and stepped aside.

As the landlady of the house, it is surprising how seldom I see the quarters of my tenants. But as each lodger is responsible for the cleaning of his or her own rooms, it is only when someone is about to move out that I have occasion to view them. I had decided long ago that I would not be one of those busybody land-ladies who intruded upon the privacy of her boarders. Ironic, of course, given the detective sideline I am in.

Mrs. Hobbs's room was much like the lady herself—bright, extravagantly furnished, cluttered, yet comfortable.

"I was hoping you could be of some assistance," I began, sitting upon a wingback chair draped with a gaudy peacock-print shawl. "As you know, Miss Leigh and I are leaving for the Adirondacks tomorrow and will be gone for a week. I find my wardrobe is less than adequate for the holiday. Might I borrow some pieces from your collection?"

She clasped her hands in delight. "Oh, I would be happy to help! Madame Violette hinted that you wished to make a change." She squinted at me intently. "I love what you have done with your hair, if you don't mind my saying so."

I smiled politely. Mrs. Hobbs had difficulty curbing both her enthusiasm and her tongue. I touched my hair self-consciously, wondering how much of a compliment it truly was. After all, the woman wasn't wearing her spectacles at the moment.

She jumped up and flung open the armoire, pulling out a gaily checked, terracotta Cheviot dress and matching bonnet. "I also have the perfect summer skirt—light as a feather. Ideal for a picnic." She poked her head between the hangers. "Where is it...."

The next half hour was spent standing before the looking glass holding up skirts, dresses, jackets, and shirtwaists. I had to admit that several items in the lady's wardrobe were actually flattering on me and not as gaudy as I had feared, such as the ecru Chantilly lace over rose silk. Perhaps, once this assignment was over, I might purchase a skirt or shirtwaist in a brighter color.

Finally, I took my leave. Cassie was busy packing, and Sadie needed a hand in the kitchen. "Thank you for the loan, Mrs. Hobbs." I shifted the pile in my arms. How I was to fit all of this into two suitcases was beyond me.

"My pleasure," the lady gushed. "I would be happy to consult with you on any future wardrobe purchases you wish to make. Perhaps we could go shopping together when you return?"

I suppressed a grimace. "Splendid."

CHAPTER 4

I had ample time to re-examine Mr. Pinkerton's notes during the three days of railway travel to reach Riparius, after which we were to catch a stagecoach to Pottersville and then the steamboat along Schroon Lake to Bittern Point and the inn.

It was not much of a report, as Pinkerton had not the benefit of firsthand information. Everything he knew came from Meyer. I re-read the bare-bones list.

Staff residing at the inn at the time of jewel thefts: Mrs. Davis, housekeeper; Mrs. Cheevy, cook; Dotty, cook's assistant; Maggie and Martha O'Neal, maids (since dismissed).

Living in cottages on the grounds: Joshua Taggart, stable master and wilderness guide, along with son Lucas, stable boy. Zeke Parker, gardener, occupies another cottage.

I turned the page. Mr. Pinkerton had listed several townspeople who were friends of Jacob Meyer or had business dealings with him.

Bittern Point locals associated with Schroon Lake Inn: Bernard Knox, retired circuit court judge, friend of Meyer; Dr. Gordon Marsh, town physician, also friend of Meyer; Lionel Atwater, owner of Cedar

Lodge; Mrs. Becham, proprietress of bait shop and general store; Nathan Traub, captain of the Galene.

The captain I could approach during our steamer trip and perhaps coax some local gossip from him. I wanted to learn if Meyer's hotel was truly a threat to Cedar Lodge's business prospects.

After learning some of Madame's spiritualist tricks, I knew the hauntings would not be difficult for Atwater to accomplish. He only needed a confederate at the inn—perhaps two—to create the ghostly sights and sounds. Sleepy guests and hysterics-prone ladies, primed on area legends, made for gullible targets.

I looked over at Cassie, contentedly embroidering by the light of the parlor car window. I hoped we would not encounter spectral sights and sounds during our stay.

Of course, the thefts were real enough. I glanced down the page for a description of the jewelry items.

Missing: three pieces of ladies' jewelry. A ruby choker from Lady Burton, a diamond brooch from Miss Maria Margeaux, and a pair of diamond earrings from Miss Frances Margeaux. Valuable pieces, but not irreplaceable.

I shook my head. Why bring expensive jewelry to a rustic retreat in the Adirondacks to begin with? I tucked away the paper with a sigh. Meyer's reasoning that the maids were to blame was flawed. If they were indeed responsible, what had happened to the items? Bittern Point was hardly a bustling metropolis with a pawnshop on every corner. It would be difficult to turn the pieces into cash. Of course, Atwater could have paid the maids to steal and now be in possession of the items.

In terms of opportunity and access to the guest rooms, the housekeeper had a key and was equally suspect. Another possibility was that the door locks were in poor condition. That would widen the field of suspects. During the daylight hours at a lakeside retreat, nearly everyone was out-of-doors—hiking, canoeing, fishing, riding horses, playing lawn tennis, or reading under a shady tree. Such pursuits would take them far from their rooms for lengthy periods. The groundskeeper, cook, or a local resident— any of these—could slip in unnoticed. Even another guest could be responsible, although Meyer's clientele was exceedingly wealthy, so that seemed unlikely. I would have to check the condition of the locks.

Two stops before Riparius, I picked up my carpetbag and groped for a handhold as the train took a curve. "I'm going to change." Cassie nodded and went back to her needlework.

She did more than nod when I returned, however. Her eyes widened at the sight of my ruffled blouse, fringed shawl, and bright floral skirt. "*Mercy*, you look like one of those sideshow fortune-tellers."

Given the second glances from across the aisle, Cassie was of the majority opinion. "I am playing a role," I said, with as much dignity as I could muster. The train slowed, and we gathered our belongings.

As we stepped off the platform, we clutched our hats in the wake of a cooling breeze and caught our first good look at the blue sweep of mountains in the horizon. Cassie smiled as she exhaled a deep breath. "If you have to look like that in order for us to be here, who am I to criticize?"

CHAPTER 5

*T*he porter adeptly dodged clumps of waiting passengers as he wheeled our luggage to the stagecoach waiting area. I was fumbling in my purse for a coin when Cassie touched my sleeve. "I believe someone is looking for you." She nodded toward a jacketless, short little man with armbands holding up his sleeves, carrying an envelope between ink-stained fingers. He caught sight of me and walked briskly toward us.

"Mrs. "—he glanced at the envelope—"Wynch?"

I hesitated briefly before inclining my head in acknowledgment.

"Telegram, ma'am."

I handed him a nickel and tore it open as he hurried away. It was from William Pinkerton.

JOUBERT BRINGING HEART OF FIRE. ESSENTIAL TO KEEP SAFE.

~WP

Heart of Fire? I passed it to Cassie. "Can you make sense of it? I assume he is not employing the phrase metaphysically."

Cassie's frown cleared. "Ah. I was just reading about that." She rummaged in her embroidery bag and pulled out the society page from *The Sun*.

I scanned it as the sound of coach wheels rattled toward us.

Miss Amalie Joubert on holiday in Adirondacks

Miss Amalie Joubert, the world-renowned soprano, will accompany a summer excursion party to the newly opened Schroon Lake Inn. It is rumored that the lady is recovering from a broken heart.

*Miss Joubert's name has graced these pages on several occasions, and not simply because of her magnificent voice. A great sensation was created when the dashing French businessman, M. Bernard, became enamored of the singer and presented her with a magnificent Australian opal, the like of which has not been seen. The size of a plover's egg, the stone reflects a fiery light, hence its name **Heart of Fire**. Sadly, the stone has proven more enduring than the gentleman's affections.*

Does the young lady bring her former swain's gift with her to the rustic lodge for consolation? What lady would not?

I grimaced. *What lady would not*, indeed. I should not complain, of course, as foolhardy girls such as these kept me employed. If everyone behaved prudently, then where would I be?

However, there was no denying my assignment had just gotten more complicated.

The coach ride to Pottersville was uneventful, although I had forgotten the bone-jarring effect of sitting atop a poorly-maintained carriage suspension on rutted roads. How Cassie managed to doze during the trip, I have no idea. My own mind was preoccupied with how to protect the Heart of Fire from both ghost and man.

I was so distracted, in fact, that I failed to properly secure my seating during one particularly bumpy stretch and all-but-landed in an elderly gentleman's lap.

"I beg your pardon," I said, hastily extricating myself and resuming my place.

His lips curved beneath his white push-broom mustache, and his dark gray eyes twinkled. "Not at all, Miss—?"

Remembering my adopted persona just in time, I inclined my head. "Madame Cerise."

He lifted an eyebrow. "Indeed? An unusual name. It is a pleasure to meet you, Madame. I'm Doctor Marsh."

Marsh. One of the names on my list. A local man and friend of Meyer, if I remembered correctly. Thank goodness I had not given myself away just now, or Madame Violette's tutorials would have been for naught.

Nodding toward my companion, he added, "You and your friend are on a summer excursion?"

"Yes, we'll be staying at Schroon Lake Inn."

"Ah. I know the proprietor very well," Marsh said.

I smiled politely. Time to introduce my alias. I could not employ the accent now, which was probably just as well. I'd never had much success with affected voices. "So you know of the stories? Ghostly sightings and strange noises? I wish to experience these spirit energies and learn more about them."

The doctor snorted. "Begging your pardon, Madame, but there is hardly *more* to be learned. Over-active feminine imaginations, coupled with creaky floorboards and local legends."

I kept my smile cool and assured, with a hint of pity. Just as Madame Violette had coached. "We will see, will we not?"

The *Galene* was already docked and waiting for us when we approached the pier at the southern end of Schroon Lake.

As Dr. Marsh gallantly handed Cassie and me out of the coach, I made the necessary introductions.

Cassie was quick to see Marsh's connection to the inn and played along with my cover. "Madame Cerise is most anxious to spend time at the inn." She turned to me. "I believe you have entertainments planned for the guests as well?"

Marsh's shaggy white eyebrows seemed to move of their own accord. "What sort of *entertainments?*"

I smiled. "The proprietor and I must settle the details, but he has kindly offered me accommodations in exchange for a week of evening diversions. We may even arrange a séance if the guests are interested."

"Madame is quite adept at reading tea leaves and tarot cards, too," Cassie said.

Marsh tried to turn his snort into a polite cough but did not quite succeed.

A group had gathered in front of the *Galene,* a small, steam-powered river craft. Cosmetically, it looked the worse for wear, but at least it had an upper viewing deck.

A youth slid the gangplank into place and began loading the luggage as a middle-aged man in a weather-beaten cap, dusty trousers, and scruffy fisherman's sweater jumped nimbly from the deck. He swept off his cap and bowed to the ladies. "Cap'n Traub, at yer service. Welcome aboard."

Soon we were underway, startling a group of ducks that swooped past the prow. Cassie and I stood at the railing, breathing deeply and taking in the wooded shoreline and the tranquil blue silhouette of the foothills beyond as we picked up speed. Except for the wake created by the vessel, the lake was as smooth as glass.

After ten minutes, I glanced at the captain stepping away from the wheel to turn it over to his first mate. I touched Cassie's arm. "I'll be back."

I watched Traub as he circulated among the passengers. It was easy to pick out the locals by the brief nod he would give before moving on, focusing his attention on the out-of-towners on holiday. He seemed particularly fond of engaging the ladies in conversation. I smiled to myself. Perfect. I perched upon a nearby bench and waited.

Traub soon greeted me, puffing contentedly upon his pipe. "Are ye headed to Cedar Lodge? Nice place, that."

I shook my head. "Schroon Lake Inn."

He stiffened, then adjusted his stance to assume a more casual air. "Oh? Ye may want to change yer plans, miss. They's been havin' a lick of trouble there."

I affected surprise. "What sort of trouble?"

He puffed on his pipe a bit before answering. "Ghosts."

The man definitely had a flair for the dramatic. I bit my lip to keep from laughing at the somber tone.

"It is last minute, to be sure," he went on, "but I know the proprietor of Cedar Lodge, Mr. Atwater. If ye like, I can have a word wi' him, and he can get take care of the arrangements. No trouble a'tall."

I was willing to bet dollars to doughnuts the captain received a kickback from Atwater for every passenger directed his way. I smiled sweetly. "In fact, captain, I have come for the express purpose of encountering such spirit phenomena. I am a medium, you see."

Traub's pipe clattered to the deck, and he bent to pick it up.

"But I am obliged to you, all the same," I added.

"Well, it don't make me no never mind," Traub harrumphed. "I wouldn't be messing with such foolishness. Don't say I didn't warn ye, miss."

As I stood up to rejoin Cassie, I noticed Dr. Marsh watching me intently. I suppressed a shiver. Was it simply the effect of those steely gray eyes that made me feel as if the man saw right through my pretense? With any luck, he would not be a regular at Schroon Lake Inn.

CHAPTER 6

*C*assie and I were the only two guests headed for the inn. The others—a dozen or so vacationers—stepped off the steamer and were handed into an elegant conveyance bound for Cedar Lodge.

We watched them leave, waiting patiently beside our luggage until a farm cart approached. Apparently, *all expenses paid* did not entail unnecessary luxuries.

The man who climbed down was in his mid-thirties, lean and sunburned with a full head of red hair lightened by the sun. He was accompanied by a boy of perhaps ten years old, equally tanned, but tow-headed. A brown-and-white beagle followed the child.

The man reached for a suitcase handle and nodded toward my carpetbag. "Lucas, grab that one for the lady."

The boy gave me an awkward bow and reached out a hand.

"Thank you, young man," I said, passing it over.

He ducked his head shyly and ran with it to the cart.

The man chuckled. "Don't mind him, he's a good boy. Just quiet. I'm Josh Taggart, by the way. That's my son, Lucas. Sorry to forget the niceties, but this isn't part of my usual job."

"Oh? What do you normally do around here, Mr. Taggart?" I accepted his hand and stepped up into the cart.

He shrugged as he handed Cassie onto the bench beside me. "A little of everything. Running the stable, wilderness guide.... I show the guests the best fishing spots, horse trails, picnic areas, and hiking paths."

"That's good to know," Cassie said. "We may avail ourselves of your services this week."

Taggart frowned as he settled himself in the driver's seat and flicked the reins. "I 'spect the Barrington party will be keeping me plenty busy, but you tell me what you want and I'll make sure someone helps you, even if it in't me. Mr. Meyer has hired extra staff for the week."

I leaned forward to be heard over the clattering wheels. "What sort of excursions do the Barringtons have planned?"

"A lot of fishing," he shouted back. "There's to be a canoe trip north of here to a picnic spot and fishing hole I know. Folks think Pharaoh Lake is the only place where trout are plentiful, but there's an inlet nearby that few know about. Sometimes the ladies like to come along and eat their crumpets while watching the men catch dinner."

"That sounds lovely," Cassie said wistfully, looking at me. I shook my head. We shouldn't barge in on the Barringtons' excursion.

Soon the grand pavilion of Schroon Lake Inn came into view. The inn was a four-story, elaborately trimmed wood-and-clapboard structure, with a white-columned porch that spanned the width of the building. Balconies flanked the sides, and the corniced roof sported tall dormers at each end. Cassie raised an eyebrow in appreciation.

As we circled the drive and stopped under the *porte cochère*, I could see that, just behind the left side of the porch, a tarpaulin screened that side of the house from view. The sound of hammering confirmed that Meyer's renovations were not yet complete.

"Mr. Meyer asked you to join him in the Rose Room," Taggart said. "Second door on your right. We'll bring your luggage up to your rooms."

We thanked him and headed for the Rose Room. It was aptly named, as the wallpaper above the whitewashed paneling was imprinted in a profusion of tiny rosebuds, and the rose-hued silk curtains, fringed lampshades, and deeply tufted upholstery echoed the theme. The effect was charming.

A man approached the arched doorway as we entered. "Welcome. I'm Jacob Meyer."

The balding man was barely of a height to my shoulder and exceedingly stout, his triple chins suppressed by a collar that looked none too comfortable. As he waved us into seats, he frowned over my attire and turned to Cassie. "You are Mrs. Wynch, sent by Mr. Pinkerton?"

"*I* am Mrs. Wynch," I cut in sharply. "This is my companion, Miss Leigh."

Meyer glanced between us in doubtful silence.

"Did Mr. Pinkerton not inform you of my cover story for this visit? I am here as spirit medium Madame Cerise. I would appreciate you going along with the ruse and addressing me as such in the future."

Meyer's frown deepened.

"Mrs. Wynch—Madame Cerise, I mean—is actually a respectable woman and quite skilled in her duties," Cassie interjected hastily.

I ground my teeth. The last thing I wanted was Cassie fighting my battles. I looked around the spacious parlor, assessing possible hiding places for Cassie during a séance. Both the deep, curtained window recess and oversized cabinet in the far corner looked promising.

Meyer gave a mighty sigh. "Pinkerton said there would be some subterfuge. He did not say what."

"Since stories have been circulating about the inn being haunted, it seemed plausible that a medium would be drawn to such a place. I am quite prepared to act in that capacity." At least, I hoped so. "I can read tea leaves, cards, palms...even conduct a séance if your guests so desire. It may amuse them." I shifted in my seat. It felt disconcerting to be touting my wares, so to speak.

"How does that benefit my establishment in the least?" Meyer protested. "It will only reinforce the stories."

"Only temporarily," I assured him. "Once this is cleared up, it will seem merely a publicity stunt in retrospect. However, the subterfuge is necessary. I will have greater freedom to investigate without arousing suspicion. After all, no one would bat an eyelash over a spirit medium wishing to meet a ghost."

He sighed.

"You don't want your guests to know that I am a private detective, do you?" I pressed.

In the end, Meyer agreed to play along and helped me plan an itinerary of psychic activities during my stay. "But I want no hocus-pocus tonight," he warned. "The Barringtons and their party arrive in a few hours and will be busy getting settled in. I do not want them harassed."

I sat back in astonishment. "A few hours? I was told they were coming tomorrow." Not much time to reconnoiter the house and grounds and make my arrangements.

"It was a last-minute decision. One of our guests, Mr. Kendall, is a good friend of the Barringtons and hired express coaches for the entire party."

Cassie and I exchanged a glance. The man must have deep pockets for such an expenditure.

"I'll have Mrs. Davis show you your rooms. I've put you in the second floor suite of rooms where the ghost sighting took place."

Cassie suppressed a shudder.

THE MYSTERY OF SCHROON LAKE INN

"Not that you'll find anything untoward about it," Meyer added, passing us each a key. "We've explored every nook and cranny. No secret caches or anything like that." Still, he looked troubled.

"Where did the thefts take place?" I asked.

Meyer winced. "The two second-floor guest rooms directly across the hall from yours. Lady Burton occupied the one on the left, and the Misses Margeaux to the right." He reached for the bell pull.

I stood, as did Cassie. "Did you know that Miss Joubert is bringing the rare opal, Heart of Fire, here with her?"

"What?" Meyer, slower to get out of his chair, nearly fell back upon it. "No, I did not. How do *you* know?"

"We read it in the newspaper," Cassie said.

He passed a kerchief across his shining scalp. "The newspaper...such publicity! We must convince her to put it in the safe."

I lifted a skeptical eyebrow. "Has any female guest availed herself of your safe since you installed it?"

"N-no, although one of the gentlemen lodgers is using it now."

"I very much doubt Miss Joubert will agree to keep her opal there." When a lady brings her jewels, it is for show, not to languish in the obscurity of a safe. The man was woefully ignorant of the ways of women.

He glared. "I am holding you personally accountable for the safety of that jewel, Mrs.—Madame Cerise. I did not want a mere woman to handle this in the first place. Mr. Pinkerton, however, insisted that it be you."

While I was gratified by Mr. Pinkerton's confidence in me, I gritted my teeth over *mere woman*. "Why do you worry that the Heart of Fire is at risk?" I asked. "I was told you fired the chambermaids you judged to be responsible for the previous jewel thefts."

"I—I'm not sure now." He looked down at his hands. "I may have been...hasty in that regard."

Whom did he suspect? Before I could phrase the question aloud, there was a brisk knock at the door, and a petite, trim-figured woman stepped in.

Meyer waved a hand. "This is our housekeeper, Hannah Davis. Mrs. Davis, meet Miss Leigh and Madame Cerise."

I was curious about the housekeeper, now the only other staff member besides Meyer himself who possessed a key to the rooms. Judging by her lined face and the strands of silver in her pale-blond hair, I would guess her to be in her early forties. She moved with a no-nonsense vigor that suited her profession.

The woman looked me up and down, her hazel eyes narrowing at the sight of my gaily printed floral skirt and ruffled blouse. "I reckon you're one of those spirit gypsies or some such. We been gettin' a sight more o' them lately." She glanced over at the innkeeper, shaking her head and muttering under her breath, "What you're thinkin' is beyond me, Jacob Meyer."

Either Meyer had not heard or was ignoring her. "Miss Leigh and Madame Cerise will be in the Elk Suite."

She turned on her heel. "Well, come on then!"

We followed her up the stairs. As I was at least a head taller than the woman, I had a plain view of the precise middle part of her light hair, one rebellious segment near the crown having been tamed into submission.

She flung open the first door at the top. It was a cozy space, though roomy enough for a high canopy bed, tufted rug, bureau, and sitting area beside the balcony doors. Tongue-in-groove white beadboard paneling covered the walls.

She stuck her head in and jerked a thumb at a connecting door built into the paneling. "Other room's through there. I must get back to work." And with that, she abruptly left.

Cassie hefted her suitcase, her hand on the connecting door. "Well, she's a charmer. I wonder if she ever smiles?"

I opened the balcony doors and leaned out. We were directly over the dining hall. The sounds of tables and chairs being moved about were audible over the buzzing of cicadas. "Perhaps she only disapproves of *us*." I took off my hat and smoothed my hair in front of the looking glass. "There's only a little time before the Barrington party is expected. I'm off to explore."

"What are you looking for?"

I sighed. "I wish I knew."

CHAPTER 7

$\mathcal{F}$irst on my list were the rooms where the thefts occurred. After checking the hallway, I slipped into the first room, the one Lady Burton had stayed in last week.

It didn't have a balcony, but two deep windows were open wide to air out the space. The bed was bare of linens. I would have to hurry. Someone was bound to make up the room soon. If I were caught, I had only one trick up my sleeve that Madame Violette had taught me. I would rather not use it so early.

According to Pinkerton, Meyer had made a thorough search for the jewels at the time of the loss. However, it wouldn't hurt to look again. I pushed aside the dust ruffle and ducked my head under the bed, sneezing at the dust. Mercy, had Meyer not hired replacements for the maids? If he had, the new ones left much to be desired. Dirt had been swept *under* the bed instead of out from under it.

Amid the clumps was an assortment of stray hatpins, buttons, and even a black enameled cufflink. I plucked it out and blew off the dust. Not on the list of the stolen items and certainly not valuable. Nonetheless, I put it in my pocket to hand over to the house-keeper later.

I moved on to the other room, where the Margeaux sisters had stayed. This one was similar to mine, though larger, with French doors leading to a balcony. It had already been tended to and was in much better condition. Crisp linens topped the beds, and the room was free of dust. It was quickly clear that there was nothing to be found here.

A sound outside brought me to the balcony doors. I twitched aside the eyelet curtains.

Along the far hedge, where the end of the drive met the main road, the gardener plied his clippers. Suddenly he stopped, fished in his pocket, and pulled out something too small for me to see. To my puzzlement, he crouched at the base of the shrubbery and seemed to place it there. One quick glance over his shoulder, and he hefted his shears and strode away, whistling.

I had to see what it was.

Just as I was about to hurry out of the room, I turned to find Mrs. Davis, hands on narrow hips, in the doorway. My heart sank.

I quietly slipped my hand in my skirt pocket and felt for the item Madame Violette had given me.

"And what may you be doing here?" she demanded.

I pulled my hand free, dangling a small, polished amethyst from a black silken cord. "I am testing the psychic energies of the rooms. That is part of my purpose here." I glanced back toward the windows. No sign of the gardener or anyone else. I had to get to the hedge.

Mrs. Davis's frown deepened. She did not look ready to budge.

I assumed an air of confidence I didn't quite feel as I walked toward her. "I thought Mr. Meyer had informed you about the experiments I would be conducting." I smiled. "You are welcome to assist me."

She snorted and stepped aside.

The shaded driveway was empty of people and conveyances. The silence was filled with crows chorusing in the elms and my quick footsteps crunching along the gravel. I approached the far hedge beside the main road, turning back to the house briefly to be sure I had the correct spot. Yes, there was the second story balcony. With a final glance to make sure no one observed me, I crouched at the base of the hedge and felt around.

Nothing was there.

Without a care for my blouse, I lay flat on my stomach to extend my reach. Leaf litter, stray twigs, tamped earth. Nothing unusual.

I brushed myself off, picked up a long stick, and strolled casually beside the hedge, running the stick along the underside of the shrubbery until I had nearly reached the footpath leading to the lakeshore. How had the item disappeared so quickly?

"Lose something, miss?" a male voice asked.

I whipped around to find a middle-aged gentleman looking at me with keen blue eyes. Although I had never met him before, his sweeping gray mustache beneath an aquiline nose, long, bristled muttonchops, and bright silk kerchief knotted at his neck made it obvious that he was none other than Spencer Rayburn, the game hunter. I'd seen enough caricatures of the man that he may as well have been carrying a pith helmet under his arm instead of the fishing pole he currently grasped.

I frowned. I thought he was arriving with the Barrington party. How was he here already?

"Miss?" he repeated. "Are you all right?"

"I beg your pardon. Yes, I'm fine. Daydreaming, I'm afraid." I waved my stick in the direction of the sparkling lake. "It's beautiful here."

"Indeed, it is." He gave a little bow. "Spencer Rayburn, at your service, Miss—?"

"Madame Cerise," I replied. "I didn't realize there were other guests here already, besides myself and my companion, Miss Leigh."

"Well, there's just Kendall and myself. And at the moment he is off to meet the Barringtons' train." He gave me a tobacco-stained toothy grin. "It will be good to have more guests to make the place lively. It has been rather quiet these past few days."

"You do not enjoy the tranquility, sir?"

"At times, of course. It gives me the opportunity to work on my memoir." He hesitated. "You may have heard of me—?"

"Indeed, I have. You are a game hunter, correct?"

"*Big* game," he corrected.

Just in time, I turned my snort into a cough. *Humble* he was not. "I'm sure you have no end of fascinating stories."

"Tales that would curl your hair, if you will pardon the expression, Madame. But—" He checked his watch. "I must go. Taggart is waiting for me at the dock." He bowed again. "A pleasure."

By the time I returned to the suite, Cassie had finished unpacking for both of us and had changed out of her traveling suit into a dress of cool green linen. "I was about to take a book down to the arbor. I can wait for you to change, if you'd like to join me."

I shook my head. "That sounds lovely, but I have more reconnoitering to do before the guests arrive." I nodded toward the small case on the dresser, containing Madame Violette's séance props. "I want to find a suitable table to wire and check the Rose Room again more carefully. I'm hoping that deep cabinet will be suitable to conceal you during a séance."

Cassie bit her lip. "Do you really think we can manage it without being caught?"

I patted her hand in reassurance. "Don't worry. I will take every precaution."

I took a circuitous route to Meyer's office, following the second floor corridor to the east wing of the house, then down the back stairs, through the servant's pantry and spacious kitchen. There I found a lightweight, gate-leg table that should suffice for tipping, though by my guess we could only seat six guests around it.

The door to the dining hall was locked. Exploring that room would have to wait. I went on to tour the sunroom and library, which connected at one end to the Rose Room.

Fortunately, the Rose Room was open. Yes, this space should work for a séance, as long as the lights were dimmed and we rearranged some of the furniture. The cabinet was deep enough to hide someone.

My tour complete, I approached Meyer's open office and knocked on the doorframe. Scowling, he looked up from a stack of papers atop his desk. "Yes?"

I seated myself without invitation. "I wish to know more about the timing of events here this summer."

He leaned back with a sigh.

I took that as permission to continue. "You opened for business this past May, is that correct?"

"Late May." He grimaced. "There were some—setbacks."

"Mr. Pinkerton said something about that. What sort of setbacks?"

"Tools broken or simply missing, workers not showing up as promised…. The worst was a wood shipment that the mill owner swore was canceled, although I had done no such thing."

"It sounds as if someone attempted to sabotage you from the start."

He took out his kerchief and blotted his forehead. "I have wondered."

"In the time since you opened for business, you have had a steady stream of guests?"

He shrugged. "In the beginning, at least, there were more than I could accommodate, although that will change. You may have noticed there are parts of the building not yet used."

I nodded.

"I've begun renovating those spaces as well," he went on. "By next season, we should have double the capacity."

"When did the ghostly incidents start?"

"Last month." He frowned. "Last-minute cancellations soon followed."

July. More than a month after he'd opened for business.

"You believe your rival, Lionel Atwater, is responsible for the incidents?"

Meyer shrugged. "It's the only logical explanation. He is in the position to widely circulate such rumors."

"I'd say Atwater had help circulating them." I recounted the captain's attempt to redirect me to Cedar Lodge while I was aboard the *Galene*.

Meyer's frown deepened to a scowl. "That no-good scoundrel! I should have known he was in Atwater's pocket."

"But Atwater runs a much bigger lodge. How could your early success seem such a threat to him?"

"The ghost incidents started when I began renovations to open up the east wing of the inn. He must have realized my clientele would only grow larger. From what I've seen, he's a very competitive man. Boastful. When he attended our opening reception in May, he made constant comparisons to his own lodge. Everything from the number of staff to the height of the ceilings."

"Does any of your staff have ties to Atwater?"

He sighed. "Nearly everyone. We're all interconnected here. It's unavoidable. He and I share suppliers, employees, coach drivers, and of course, the steamer captain."

No help there. "What about Mrs. Davis?"

He stiffened. "What about her?"

"Does she have any association with Atwater?"

He shook his head. "Only a passing acquaintance. You could say the same for any of us. It's a small town."

"Mr. Pinkerton mentioned she has been in your employ for quite some time."

"She has been housekeeper to me for nine years, first in New York City. She agreed to follow me up here, although she didn't care for the idea."

"Oh? Why not?"

"She used to live around here and left because it was too quiet...too isolated."

I started. Mrs. Davis was a former resident of Bittern Point.... The lady, then, may have more than a *passing acquaintance* with Atwater. I did not voice my suspicion aloud. "She must be extraordinarily devoted to you to be willing to return in spite of it."

He reddened.

I decided to change the subject. "When did the last supernatural incident take place?"

"Three nights ago, just after a dinner party."

"What happened?"

"There were sounds. Metal scraping, then a whisper. They seemed to come from the back wall of the dining room."

"And there is nothing behind the walls?"

Meyer pushed away from the desk. "Come see for yourself."

I followed him to the dining room. He unlocked the door and pushed it wide. It was massive, restaurant-sized. Meyer had an eye to expansion, for sure. Part of the space was screened off to create cozy groupings of café-style tables and chairs.

I followed his waddling form across the room. He put a hand to the back wall, flanked by recessed windows. "The sounds came from here. As you can see, there is nothing behind it."

I stuck my head out of the open window and looked at the outer wall. Sure enough, barely eighteen inches existed between the outer and inner wall. "You say your guests heard the sounds?"

Meyer shrugged. "If you mean guests at the inn, there were only two here at the time. Mr. Kendall and Mr. Rayburn, and they dined with us that evening. We all heard the sounds."

"Who else attended this dinner?"

"Judge Knox, Mrs. Becham—she's a widow who runs the

general store—Dr. Marsh, and Mrs. Davis. We were a bit out of balance when it came to the ladies, which is often the case around here. It's a paradise for fishermen and hunters, but not so much for the fairer sex."

I kept a comment to myself about the housekeeper joining a dinner party. Perhaps Meyer was trying to round out his numbers.

I returned to the subject at hand. "Tell me more about the jewel thefts. They happened last week?"

"Ten days ago, now," he said. "Lady Burton and her daughters had lost several pieces between them, and a search of their rooms had turned up nothing."

"Expensive items, I believe?" I recalled the list Pinkerton had provided.

Meyer grimaced. "Quite. Mrs. Davis and I conducted our own search. We were thorough and very discreet. Besides the common areas, we went through the quarters for the servants who sleep in —without their knowledge, of course. No luck."

"Who sleeps in?"

"Mrs. Davis, the cook, the cook's assistant, and at the time, the two maids. Sisters. The others either reside in Bittern Point or have a cottage on the grounds, as do I."

"And you dismissed the maids, without proof? Did you question them first?"

He shook his head. "Mrs. Davis felt strongly that the girls were to blame and should go. I couldn't risk word getting out about the loss. So I dismissed them, saying I was dissatisfied with their work. They *were* rather lazy. We are making do with day help now."

"What do you think happened to the jewels after they were stolen?"

"Atwater has them, I'm sure of it. I cannot prove it, of course."

I frowned. If Atwater was behind it, then why did he not

spread the rumor of the jewel thefts? That would deter guests more effectively than a ghost.

The sound of carriage wheels on the gravel drive reached our ears.

"Ah, that must be the Barrington party." Meyer tugged at his vest and rolled down his sleeves. "If you will excuse me, Madame."

CHAPTER 8

*C*urious about the newcomers but not wanting to get in the way, I passed through the sunroom, followed the path around the side of the building, and took up a position on a bench in the latticed arbor overlooking the side gardens and front pavilion. Servants stood beside two carriages, handing out passengers. Taggart and his son had climbed atop a third carriage piled high with luggage and were busy untying the ropes.

I watched Jacob Meyer as he greeted his guests with that perfect blend of dignity and servility that marks the successful innkeeper. As the first guests he greeted were a stooped, gray-haired gentleman and the erect-carriaged older woman on his arm, I assumed they were the Barringtons. A slim, dark-haired man in his thirties followed behind. He possessed a strong chin and dimples that creased his cheeks when he smiled, and carried himself with the ease of one who knows he can command the admiration of the opposite sex.

The dimples were in full view as he smiled avidly at the curvaceous young lady beside him, chatting with the ease of long acquaintance as he guided her up the steps. I recognized the full-lipped, dark-eyed beauty at his side. Amalie Joubert, the opera singer. She was dressed in a simple traveling suit of pale blue gabardine, a froth of white lace at the throat and cuffs. She wasn't wearing the Heart of Fire gemstone at the moment. Not surprising, of course—one does not wear such a piece while traveling. I should know by dinner this evening if the lady had brought it along.

Several guests were exiting the second carriage. Another middle-aged couple, along with two girls of debutante years and a college-aged youth. I didn't recognize any of them.

"Ah, I see we no longer have the place to ourselves."

I turned to see Cassie propped against the arbor railing, book in hand.

"Do you know any of them?" I asked. Cassie came from a family even better connected than the Hamiltons. "I only recognize the singer."

She nodded toward the group, now heading inside. "Mama knows the Barringtons—the couple walking in with Meyer."

I straightened hastily. "Not well, I hope." I did not want society gossip to give away my cover.

Cassie laughed. "The Barringtons are too stuffy, even for Mama."

I discreetly pointed to the dark-haired man. "What about him?"

Her face brightened. "Oh my, he's a handsome one. That must be Phillip Kendall. The maid who brought me tea was sighing over one of the guests already here. He fits her description."

Looking at the way Cassie couldn't take her eyes off the man, I wondered if she was doing a little sighing herself. That could be trouble. The gentleman in question looked as if he was accustomed to the company of exotic beauties. To be sure, Cassie was quick-witted and charming, with a ready smile and pleasant features, but exotic she was not.

I watched them go in. "This should be an interesting evening." I was determined to make it so.

Back in our suite, I was soon dressed and ready for dinner. My silk dress of midnight blue had been shaken out and hung up hours before and was easy to slip into. I'd also become more adept at the braided coronet arrangement that Madame Violette had devised for my hair. A tuck here, an extra pin there, and I was done. At the last minute, I decided to add the pearl-crusted hair comb Madame had seen fit to lend me. "It resembles a tiara, and gives you a more regal look," she had said. "Remember, you believe you were a princess in another life. You must act the part."

Cassie was dressed in her finest taffeta of Nile green. She grimaced at her reflection. "I should have worn a broad-brimmed hat today." She put a hand to her freckled, reddened neck.

Poor girl, she *does* freckle quickly in the sun. "Wait, I have just the thing." I crossed back to my room and pulled a gauzy scarf of dotted ivory from the drawer. "Try this."

After some artistic draping, Cassie was pleased with the result. She squeezed my hand in gratitude. "Perfect."

"Anyone in particular you seek to impress? A certain tall, dark gentleman, perhaps?" I teased.

She laughed. "Can you blame me?"

"Not at all, as long as he is worthy of you. We shall see." I kept my tone light as I picked up my gloves. "Ready?"

Because of the uncertainty of the exact time of the guests' arrival, dinner had been planned as a buffet meal. Meyer elected not to dine with us this evening. I felt distinctly over-dressed, wishing I had saved the hair comb for tomorrow evening. Ah well, once a princess, always a princess, I suppose.

There was another drawback to the arrangement—Cassie and I were left to a table by ourselves while the Barringtons and their friends mingled and shared tables. We had made the acquaintance of the new arrivals, of course. Indeed, there had been a few eyebrows raised when I was introduced as the clairvoyant Madame Cerise. Perhaps that was why no one sought our company during the meal.

I noted Cassie's crestfallen look. "Tomorrow's dinner will be more formal," I said. "We should all be seated together then."

She nodded and poked a fork at her veal cassoulet.

As I ate, I surveyed the room, observing who conversed with whom. My eyes strayed frequently to Miss Joubert. The lady was indeed wearing the Heart of Fire opal. The pendant dropped low, just past her décolletage. Even from a distance, it was an astonishing piece, catching the light with orange-red bursts as she moved.

The young people naturally gravitated toward one another and had a table to themselves. Free of parental impediment, they made a gay little group. Constance Barrington laughed at her brother Charles's antics, as he attempted to twist a napkin into a rose for the blushing Evelyn Holloway.

The parents paid little heed to their youngsters, conversing quietly at a nearby table. Mr. Barrington frequently cleared his throat. Perhaps the food did not agree with him. The veal *was* a bit spicy.

Miss Joubert, Mr. Kendall, and Mr. Rayburn occupied the table closest to us, just beneath the window, and seemed the most animated in the room. Cassie and I shamelessly eavesdropped upon Rayburn's account of hunting a man-eating tiger in Champawat.

"Over the years, the beast had killed at least three hundred villagers in the area and had not been captured," he said, smoothing his mustache and sitting back in his chair. "I'm glad to say I was finally able to get him. Took months of tracking. We dug many a spiked pit."

Miss Joubert shuddered. "Still, it seems so cruel."

Rayburn smiled and shook his head. "It was a necessity. Once a tiger gets a taste for human meat, there's no stopping it."

Mr. Kendall leaned forward, glancing anxiously at the pale-faced Miss Joubert. "Here now, let us change the subject. We don't wish to distress the lady with such grim matters." She gave him a grateful look.

I sighed. I would have enjoyed hearing more. Perhaps I wasn't as ladylike as the singer.

Mrs. Barrington and Mrs. Holloway were being helped out of their chairs. Time to retire to the drawing room for after-dinner coffee and cordials.

As if on cue, Mrs. Davis hurried in, followed by several wait staff, who busied themselves re-laying the buffet with port and cigars for the gentlemen.

"The Rose Room is ready, ladies," Mrs. Davis said. "Allow me to show you the way."

The shadows of dusk stretched across the room. A maid turned up the lamps as we settled ourselves, then began pouring coffee and sherry.

I caught Mrs. Davis on her way out. "Could you please bring me tea instead?"

She sniffed.

I sat upon the divan beneath the window, Cassie beside me. Soon the housekeeper returned with a tea tray. "Ah, thank you," I said.

"You wish tea as well, Miss Leigh?" Mrs. Davis asked.

Cassie glanced my way. "If you please, Mrs. Davis."

The housekeeper produced another cup, poured, and left.

I drained my cup quickly as the ladies chatted, then spilled the leaves from my cup into the saucer. I was flouting Meyer's embargo on "hocus-pocus" tonight, but I didn't have much time. Besides, he wasn't here.

I muttered a few exotic words as I stared into the saucer, catching Miss Joubert's attention. She leaned across the low table.

I pretended not to notice. Cassie set down her cup, turning toward us for maximum effect.

"What is it you're doing?" Miss Joubert asked.

I tipped the saucer this way and that to catch the light. "Reading the leaves."

The lady gestured excitedly. "So you see certain patterns—" Her ring caught in the long chain of her pendant. "*Bother*," she muttered. She took off the necklace and set it aside on the tray.

I eyed the pendant briefly before turning my attention back to the saucer. "Indeed, yes, and there is significance to the shapes I see." I nudged one of the clumps gently with a fingernail. "This one, you see it? It is a pistol, which signifies danger. There is a star next to it. The star is a psychically powerful symbol. Just as I had expected."

Miss Joubert frowned. "What do you mean?"

"Have you heard about the spirit manifestations in this household?"

Cassie nodded vigorously. "I have. It is said that the ghost of the previous owner—his name escapes me at the moment—lingers here, at the inn." She shivered.

Misses Holloway and Barrington, catching part of the conversation, drew their chairs closer.

I tapped the saucer. "This predicts that I will experience a visitation tonight." Cassie shivered again. I was sure it was genuine this time.

At that moment, the door swung open. Miss Barrington let out a little squeak, but it was only the gentlemen joining us, the housekeeper following with more coffee.

Cassie finished her tea and held out the cup. "Madame Cerise, would you mind reading my cup next?"

Perfect. Bless the girl for rising to the occasion.

"Of course."

We had the attention of most of the room now. All of the

ladies except Mrs. Barrington waylaid Mrs. Davis for tea instead of coffee.

I leaned back to catch my breath and let my gaze wander. It was not completely dark outside yet. Through the window, I could just make out the far hedge and a bit of the road beyond. A wagon clattered past, slowed and stopped. After a moment, it moved on.

What was that about? The hedge again. I suppressed a sigh. It would have to wait. As dearly as I wanted to know what was going on, I was committed to an evening of tea-leaf readings.

The men looked on in a mixture of amusement and derision as we ladies sipped tea, chatted, and examined the leaves. I took Madame Violette's advice to heart, mixing prognostications of love and good fortune with warnings of possible deception and loss.

I had Miss Joubert in mind in terms of the latter when I picked up her cup, tipping it this way and that, frowning.

"What do you see?" she asked anxiously.

"I see a past sadness, here in the shape of a broken ring," I said slowly, recalling the society page article about a faithless suitor. The lady blushed and glanced down at her hands. Phillip Kendall stepped closer, looking over her shoulder.

"But this heart shape, it is a very good sign of an impending courtship," I went on, sloshing the bits around.

Kendall perched on a settee to the lady's right. Spencer Rayburn, closing in on the hunt, sat to her left. The man absolutely reeked of cigar smoke.

I glanced briefly at the pendant on the tray amid the litter of cups, saucers, and spoons before turning back to the leaves. "However...you see the purse?"

She squinted doubtfully. "I'm not sure... Oh yes, I see it now. What does that mean?"

I sighed. "It depends upon its position within the cup. A purse can signify profit, but unfortunately when it's at the bottom of the cup as it is here, it indicates you will suffer a loss. I would guard your valuables quite closely, Miss Joubert."

"Oh!" She grabbed the pendant, clasping it tightly upon the napkin in her lap.

I hid a smile. Good. Perhaps my job just got a bit easier.

The group broke up shortly afterward, Spencer and Holloway electing to go to the billiard room, the young people heading down to the lake for a bonfire, the others retiring for the night.

Cassie hesitated on the stair when I didn't follow. "Coming up?"

I shook my head. "I'm going out for a little fresh air. Goodnight."

Drat. I'd forgotten my shawl in the Rose Room. I stepped around Mrs. Davis and the maid clearing up the dishes. "You made quite a mess for us to clean up," the housekeeper said testily over her shoulder.

I shrugged in apology, grabbed my shawl, and slipped out.

I hadn't realized how stuffy it had become in the Rose Room until I was outside. The night air was blessedly cool and bracing. The pavilion drive was ringed with hanging lanterns, but all beyond was dark. I helped myself to one of the lights and continued down the driveway to the road.

No one was about, although I heard the rustling of some animal in the shrubbery and the hoot of an owl. Even with a light, that I would not be able to see very far. I walked along the deserted road, the hedge that bordered the property as high as my shoulder. The road was graveled rather than simple packed earth. Probably an expense Meyer had considered worthwhile with all of the traffic he anticipated. I crossed the road and climbed the rise, looking back at the inn.

The left flank of the building was closed to guests, under renovation for Meyer's future expansion plans. A small, rutted drive curled along that side, probably where men and materials gathered for the construction work. I'd heard some muffled hammering when I had gone down the servants' staircase earlier today. Fortunately for Meyer, it was nothing obtrusive to bother the guests. All was quiet now. Nothing looked untoward or out of place.

It seemed I could accomplish no more out-of-doors tonight. On my way back, I decided to cut through the rose garden walk, which was lined with merry Chinese lanterns and comfortable benches. Inhaling the pleasant scent of roses before bed would be most welcome. I missed my garden back home, small as it was.

"I didn't think I would see you again." The male voice was so close I nearly jumped. It was Phillip Kendall, just beyond the lattice of climbing roses to my left. I shamelessly stopped to listen. I had a good idea to whom he was speaking.

"Indeed, it had not been my plan." The breathy, high-pitched tones were those of Miss Joubert. I nodded to myself. It didn't take a clairvoyant to know that something was going on between those two.

"I could not believe it when you ran off with that...Frenchman."

"I did not *run off*." The lady's voice rose in her indignation. "You know I had performances in Paris those two months. And you were occupied with a certain Southern belle. I read all about it."

"All right, all right, I admit it. I made a mistake." I could barely hear the next words. "...where we left off? We are well suited, you know."

At first, there was silence, then the resounding, unmistakable sound of a *slap*. The shrubbery beside the lattice rustled in agitation. As hurried footsteps came my way, I ran for the side door to escape observation.

I was calmly reading in an alcove in view of the lobby by the time Amalie Joubert entered. She blew out a breath and self-consciously smoothed her hair at the sight of me.

"Good evening," she said, with exaggerated calm.

As she passed close to the light of my reading lamp, my eyes strayed to her throat, checking for the chain of her pendant.

It wasn't there.

A chill of apprehension plucked at my spine, but I kept my voice calm. "Where is your opal, Miss Joubert?"

She raised a hand to her neck. Her eyes widened. "I-I must have left it in the Rose Room."

I set my book aside. "I'll help you look."

Kendall entered the foyer and stopped at the sight of us. "Something wrong?"

"Miss Joubert has mislaid her jewel."

He joined us in the search of the Rose Room. "I last saw it when you picked it up from the tea table." He grunted as he groped beneath a chair cushion.

I nodded, dropping to my hands and knees to feel under the table. "That's what I remember. She was holding it in her lap." I could kick myself for not attending to it after that. I'd been in too much of a hurry to end the session and check the road beyond the hedge.

I am holding you personally accountable for the safety of that jewel, Meyer had said.

I could be in serious trouble.

"What's going on here?" Spencer Rayburn stood in the doorway, cigar in hand, shaggy brows drawn together.

We seemed to be drawing a crowd. "Miss Joubert's opal is missing."

"Really?" Rayburn set down his cigar in the ashtray. "How unfortunate. Can I help?"

Kendall ignored him completely. "What else do you remember?" he asked the singer. "Perhaps you put it in a skirt pocket?"

I glanced at Miss Joubert, eyebrow raised, and she met my look. *Men.*

She stopped just short of rolling her eyes. "You gentlemen may have such conveniences in *your* evening attire. We ladies, however, do not." She sighed. "I must have set it aside again without thinking. The chain kept catching on things, so I didn't put it back on."

"I noticed the housekeeper and maid clearing the dishes a little while ago," I said. "Perhaps you left it in a napkin, where it escaped notice and was tossed in the linen hamper. We should ask Mrs. Davis."

As if seeing me for the first time, Mr. Kendall gave me a warm look of appreciation that made me blush in spite of myself. "Good thinking, Madame."

"I'll go fetch her," Rayburn offered, hurrying down the hall toward the kitchen.

Kendall patted the hand of the distraught Miss Joubert. "Don't worry. We'll find it."

Unfortunately, Mrs. Davis had sent out the table linens to be cleaned. "Those are heirloom textiles," she snapped, hands on hips, glaring in my direction. "After all your tea-leaf-reading nonsense, I knew the napkins and tray-cloth would need special cleaning. There's a woman in Bittern Point who works wonders with stains." After a glance at Miss Joubert's stricken expression, she softened her tone. "Try not to worry, miss. Granny Aubry is as honest as the day is long. If your necklace was bundled in there, she'll keep it safe for you. I'll send a messenger in the morning."

The search party broke up after that, Rayburn heading for the library and the rest of us climbing the stairs to our rooms. Kendall accompanied Miss Joubert to her door down the corridor from mine. I smothered a yawn as I turned the door key. Well, I *tried* to turn it. The key wouldn't budge. "*Bother.*"

The ever-perceptive Phillip Kendall was by my side in an instant. "Trouble, Madame? Here, allow me." He jiggled the key free, reinserted it, then lifted up on the knob as he twisted. "There's a trick to these old locks," he laughed.

I looked up at him—Kendall was one of the few men taller than I. His deep brown eyes crinkled at the corners with bright good humor. He was standing so close I could pick up the scent of his bay-rum aftershave. Oh yes, this man could be trouble. Little wonder Cassie found him attractive.

"Good night." I slipped into my room and closed the door firmly behind me.

I could hear his low whistle as he took the stairs up to his third floor room.

I turned up the lamp, giving my bed a longing look. That would have to wait. I must write an entry in my logbook for the day, and I had not had the opportunity to explore the room. I wasn't about to take Meyer at his word that he had thoroughly searched for hidden recesses. Our ghost had to come from somewhere.

The connecting door to Cassie's room was closed. No light showed beneath. I would have to check her room tomorrow.

After writing a log entry, I spent the next hour tapping and running my hands along the paneling. I lifted the throw rug and looked under the bed, searching for a hatch or trap door. Nothing. I stepped out onto the tiny balcony to check for nearby vegetation by which one could gain access. The surrounding area was bare.

The breeze from the lake tugged at my hair in its pins. I released the braid and began to unravel it, running my fingers through my scalp with a sigh.

There wasn't much to see from my vantage point. The outside lights had been extinguished, and the house was shut up for the night. Through the tall pines, I could make out the faintest glimmer of moonlight on the waters of Schroon Lake.

I heard a step on the balcony overhead and smelled a burning cigar. Spencer Rayburn, no doubt. I had only a vague idea of who else occupied which rooms on the third floor. That would be one of my tasks for tomorrow. In the meantime, my bed beckoned to me.

CHAPTER 9

J was never sure what woke me that night. All I know is I opened my eyes, momentarily disoriented as I stared at the medallioned-tin ceiling overhead. Then I remembered where I was.

I glanced at the mantel clock, illuminated by the hurricane lamp. Three in the morning. I sat up and listened. The sound of tree frogs drifted through the open window. Nothing more.

Something had awoken me, and it certainly wasn't frogs. I slipped on my dressing gown and slippers and stepped out on the balcony. The moon had risen higher, illuminating the still grounds below in a cold white light. I shivered.

I was about to go back inside when a shadow moved among the pines. No, *two* shadows. I leaned against the railing for a better look. If I didn't miss my guess, it was Miss Holloway, accompanied by Charles Barrington. *Oh-ho-ho*, the parents would do well to keep a closer eye on those two. Perhaps a well-placed hint from a clairvoyant would do the trick.

As I stood in the room, trying to determine what to do next, I heard a dull, metallic *scrape* that sent a prickle of unease along my spine.

I took a deep breath. *Ghosts are not real.*

I ran to the wall behind my bed and put my ear to it. Yes, there it was again. The sound was faint, echoing from below. Below... what was below? The dining room.

I opened my door with barely a sound, thanks to the knob trick Kendall had shown me. I decided to leave my lamp behind. The moonlight was shining brightly through the stairwell window.

I hurried down to the dining room—mercifully not locked— and put my ear to the same back wall. Yes, it was stronger here, the sound of something heavy being pushed. Then footsteps and a whisper. I couldn't tell if it was male or female.

Was there a basement below? I had to find out.

After exploring the entire ground floor of the inn, I could find no door leading to an underground basement. If there was one, the access must be from outside. I headed for the back door in the kitchen.

"Madame?" a husky voice whispered.

I stifled a shriek, whipping around to see Spencer Rayburn, still in his evening attire, looking me up and down with a puzzled frown. I self-consciously tightened the sash of my dressing gown.

"You're not still looking for Miss Joubert's opal, I hope? I'm sure it will be recovered."

"No, not at all. I heard something."

He raised an eyebrow. "Ghost-hunting, Madame? I would have thought you'd be more, *ahem*, suitably attired for the occasion."

I stiffened. "One cannot control the time when ghosts appear, Mr. Rayburn. What are *you* doing up at this hour? Did you hear something as well?"

He chuckled. "Hardly. I've been occupied with writing an account of my most recent hunt. I'm calling it 'The Ferocious Tiger of Champawat.'"

I suppressed a grimace at the melodramatic title.

"I came down for a glass of milk," he went on.

My lips twitched at the notion of The Milk-Drinking Tiger-Hunter of Champawat. Now *that* would be an intriguing title. I would read that.

The chill air plucking at my ankles brought me back from my frivolous imaginings. "Do you know if the inn has a basement?"

"I noticed a root cellar." He waved toward the kitchen door. "Just beyond there."

I poked my head out the door. Yes, so there was. Cloud cover had dimmed the moonlight by now, but I could make out the wooden hatch doors and a stout padlock. No one could have gone through there without leaving it unlocked behind him. There must be another entrance.

Rayburn was pulling a glass out of the cupboard. "Do you care for a glass of milk as well, Madame?"

I shook my head with a smile. "Thank you, no. Goodnight."

CHAPTER 10

I awoke to a knock on the connecting door and the sun shining full on my face. "Come in." I propped myself on the bed. Mercy, I'd fallen asleep with my dressing gown and slippers still on.

Cassie walked in. "You're not dressed yet? It's nine o'clock already."

"It was a rough night." I ducked behind the dressing screen and told her about Miss Joubert's missing opal as I changed into a box-pleated, striped silk of red and white. Perfect for a picnic, as Mrs. Hobbs had said. Out of sheer habit, I groped in the pockets of yesterday's skirt and blindly transferred their contents into this one.

Cassie sucked in a breath. "Meyer made you personally responsible for the jewel."

I sighed. "I know."

"And you say you searched the Rose Room?"

"Several of us searched. Mr. Rayburn and Mr. Kendall happened to be on hand and helped Miss Joubert and myself. We were thorough. It wouldn't hurt to look again, but I believe it more likely the jewel was caught up in the linens that were sent out." I fervently hoped so.

"What if a maid found it and kept it?" Cassie asked. "As disagreeable as the notion is, it must be considered."

"True enough. I'm sure Mrs. Davis has informed Meyer by now. He has no doubt questioned the staff." I grimaced. As long as he didn't fire any more of them. I couldn't imagine the Barringtons making their own beds. "But that's not all that happened last night." I described the strange noises.

Cassie grew pale.

"I'm convinced that flesh-and-blood men are behind whatever is going on here," I reassured her. "Let's go to breakfast. I'm famished."

The morning meal was being served in the sunroom, where the young Misses Holloway and Barrington were spreading marmalade on their toast and sharing a copy of *Harper's*. There was no sign of the Barrington brother or the parents.

Miss Joubert joined us a short time later. The shadows beneath her eyes indicated a sleepless night.

Mrs. Davis, carrying a towel-wrapped teapot, came over to fill our cups. "I sent Lucas into town," she said, eyes on Miss Joubert. "I will let you know as soon as he gets back."

Meyer came in right behind her. He scowled briefly in my direction before making an awkward bow before the singer. "I'm profoundly sorry to learn your jewel has been mislaid. I want to assure you we are doing everything we can to find it."

Miss Joubert choked back a sob. "It—it was the only thing from Henri that I have left—" The youngsters looked over at us.

I drew Miss Joubert's arm through mine and coaxed her from the table. "Let us find a place more private." Cassie got up and patted the lady's other hand.

Meyer's brows drew together in distress. "Yes, yes, of course." He gestured to the housekeeper. "Would you refresh the lady's plate and cup and bring them to the Rose Room?"

After Miss Joubert had been settled upon a comfortably padded armchair and Cassie and I sat together upon the afghan-draped settee, Meyer leaned toward the lady. "I have questioned the staff, but no one has seen it. When do you last remember having the gem?"

Miss Joubert sniffed. "I held it in my lap while we were finishing our tea last night. That's all I remember."

I nodded. "That is the last time I saw it, as well." Again, I wished I had paid more attention after that, but the wagon stopping in the road had distracted me.

Meyer sighed. "We shall have to wait for the boy to return. I am confident the laundress has found it by now."

Miss Joubert clasped her hands in her lap. "I do hope you're right, Mr. Meyer, but I am uneasy." She turned to me with pleading eyes. "Madame, could you use your powers to find my opal?"

My eyes widened. Madame Violette had not prepared me for *this*. "Perhaps we should wait for news."

Meyer's eyes were mocking beneath his heavy brows. "Why wait, Madame? I do not personally believe in such things, but I am not above using whatever means necessary to secure the gem. I am sure it would ease the lady's mind."

I felt Cassie shift uneasily. I understood her concern. There was no way to come out of this advantageously. If I predicted the boy had the gem and he did not, Miss Joubert and the other guests would keep me at arm's length as a silly charlatan for the rest of my stay. If I said he did not have the gem, then where would I say it was? More importantly, where was it really?

Drat, the wide belt of my skirt was digging into my back. I adjusted my position, pushing my hand against the cushion.

Wait. That was not my belt. There was something wedged there, beneath the afghan. In a flash of intuition, I knew what it was.

I had to work hard to suppress a grin. Why not take advantage of the opportunity, while wiping the smug look from Meyer's face?

"Ah, Miss Joubert, I sympathize with your distress," I said. "I am happy to help you." I made a show of extricating a deck of cards from my reticule. *The cards are your friends, good for nearly any emergency,* Madame Violette had said. I hoped they would serve me now. I casually pushed my reticule out of the way, wedging it nearly behind me on the settee and exploring the space with my fingers. I felt the bulge again behind the afghan and gave it a discreet nudge. It silently dropped through the gap to the carpeted floor underneath. That would do.

I dealt the cards, inventing the significance of the array to suit my purposes. In spite of himself, Meyer leaned forward as eagerly as Miss Joubert. I glanced through the window to my left. The Taggart boy was running up the path. Time to end the session.

"Your gem, it is very close, miss," I intoned. I closed my eyes briefly. "Yes, I feel it."

Miss Joubert clasped her hands in excitement. "Where?"

"It makes no sense...but the spirits are never wrong." I paused.

"*Where?*" Meyer thundered.

I stood, turned, and pointed beneath the settee. Cassie gave a little shriek and jumped to her feet, as if expecting ghostly hands to reach up and grab her.

Meyer pushed the settee away from the wall, awkwardly dropped to his knees, and groped. He pulled out the wadded napkin with shaking hands. We watched as he spread it out on the table. There was the pendant, besmirched by tea leaves but otherwise intact.

"My opal! Oh, thank goodness." Miss Joubert wiped it clean and put the chain over her head. "Oh, Madame Cerise, thank you. Thank you!"

I shook my head with a smile. "I was merely the conduit. Count yourself favored by the spirits, miss. They have restored it to you. It was not there before. Remember? You and I, along with

Mr. Kendall and Mr. Rayburn, searched this room thoroughly last night."

"As did Mrs. Davis, after everyone had retired," Meyer snapped, narrowing his eyes.

"Well, it doesn't matter now." Miss Joubert's smile was wide. "I have it back, and I promise to take very good care of it."

"It would be prudent to keep it in the safe," Meyer said.

The lady smiled and shook her head. With a final wave of thanks, she left, passing by Lucas, who panted for breath as he entered the room.

"But—" he started to say to her back. "We couldn' find it...."

I pulled out a coin for him. "Don't worry, the gem has been recovered. Here is something for your trouble."

Lucas grinned and tucked it away.

"Run along now," Meyer said to the boy. "And Miss Leigh, if you will excuse us? I wish to speak with Madame alone."

Cassie locked worried eyes with me before leaving the room.

I resumed my seat, and Meyer closed the door. "Now then, I will only say this once. You are *leaving* this inn. Tomorrow, if I can arrange your transportation."

My mouth hung open. "What? I have just recovered your guest's valuable jewel, and you are dismissing me?"

"That is precisely why. *You* stole the opal, just so you could stage these clairvoyant...shenanigans. What game are you playing? You're supposed to be a detective. You certainly aren't acting like one."

"If I were acting like one, that would not be much of a cover, would it?" I retorted. "You wanted discretion. I merely employed a bit of histrionics to reinforce my position here at the inn." I stood. He took a step back as I towered over him. "I did *not* steal the lady's necklace, but two disturbing possibilities spring to mind. Either it was carelessly left behind and a member of your staff succumbed to temptation, or one of your guests took it."

"Then why was it under the furniture?"

I decided to omit where I'd originally discovered it. That part didn't matter. "Obviously the perpetrator thought better of the deed. The gem is too valuable and too well known. It would attract notice as soon as someone tried to sell it. So the thief snuck back in—likely during the night or early this morning—placing it nearby so that we'd assume it had been overlooked. This room is not locked?"

Meyer shook his head. "No need. There is nothing valuable in here."

"Exactly."

He narrowed his eyes. "Why would one of the guests steal the necklace? They certainly don't need the money."

I sighed. "That is what I must discover."

$\mathcal{F}$inally, Meyer conceded the logic of my argument, muttered a gruff apology of sorts, and permitted me to stay. I left him brooding in the Rose Room, staring distractedly out the window.

I was relieved to be able to continue with my assignment and gratified to have found Miss Joubert's opal. However, several questions remained. Who had stolen it? When was it replaced? And, more importantly, would someone try again, with another lady's jewels?

If the opal had not turned up, I would have suspected the cleaning staff. How easy it would have been for someone to come upon it wrapped inside a napkin and then slip it into a pocket.

But with the opal returned, the field of suspects had thinned. The maids and wait staff did not sleep in. True, they were here early to cook and lay tables for breakfast, but a detour to the Rose Room when people were bustling about would have drawn too much attention. The most likely possibility was that someone returned the gem during the night or very early morning, before anyone was up. Mrs. Davis could have done it easily. I would have to consider that.

My instincts, however, were pointing me to Spencer Rayburn. He had been fully dressed and prowling the ground floor in the wee hours, with not much of an excuse for his presence. Perhaps he was not as affluent as he seemed. Those big-game hunts were expensive endeavors. What sort of bounty had he collected after killing the Tiger of Champawat? Enough to defray the costs? The hunter would bear watching.

At least the opal was safe. Miss Joubert wasn't likely to be careless with it in the near future. I could turn my attention to the mysterious noises I'd heard last night.

I went back to my room to retrieve my sturdy walking shoes. A note from Cassie was propped against the mirror. *Joining the boating party. Back before tea-time.*

I smiled to myself, happy that Cassie was being included in the guest activities.

I nearly collided with Lucas on my way out the front door, the dog by his side.

"Sorry, miss." The child tugged respectfully at his cap brim. The beagle came over and put his front paws on my skirts. Lucas pulled him off. "Down, boy."

I hesitated. Inquisitive boys knew all of the tucked-away places. "Tell me, does the root cellar extend very far beneath the inn?"

He shook his head. "It's jes' for vegetables, miss. It doesn't even go much under the kitchen."

"Is there a basement of any kind beneath the inn?"

The boy bit his lip. "You wouldn' want to be going in there. It's dark and damp. Kinda smells bad, too."

I took a breath to slow my quickening pulse. So, there was something. "I see. What is it used for?"

"Nothing that I can tell. I think somebody's used it, a'fore Mr. Meyer owned the place." He shrugged. "There's only old crates and such now."

"I thought I heard someone down there last night."

The boy nodded solemnly. "Ghosts," he whispered.

I fished a coin from my pocket and held it up. "I am interested in ghosts. That is why I'm here."

His eyes grew wide. "Papa told me. It seems a mighty peculiar thing to be interested in, beggin' your pardon, miss."

I put the coin in his hand. "I would much appreciate it if you showed me how to get to the cellar."

He looked me over thoughtfully. "You'd get awful mucky in that dress."

"I'll take that chance. I'm ready if you are."

I had expected some sort of hidden door alongside the building, so I was quite surprised when Lucas led me past the rose garden, along a steep, descending path that ended at the lake. As we walked, he tossed a stick to the dog, who ran back with it to do it again, over and over.

"He's tireless," I laughed, as the dog nudged him to throw it again. "What's his name?"

"Jack."

"Well, Jack, it's a pleasure to meet you." The beagle gave a little *yip*.

Just before we reached the lake, the boy veered off the path toward a pile of boulders that overlooked the shore. Vegetation cascaded from the crevices. I huffed along behind.

He clambered easily over the lower boulders, pushed aside a curtain of vines, then reached a hand down to me. "In here."

Wary of bats and spiders, I hesitated at the opening. I craned my neck around the boulders, to look up the path we had just come. We must be about five hundred yards from the building. "*This* leads to the cellar beneath the inn?"

He nodded. "But Mr. Meyer didn't build it. It's old. I found it last year."

"Is this the only way to get in?'

"Well, it's the only way *I* know."

He reached into a niche, pulling out a lantern and matches.

"You are a resourceful young man," I said, ducking my head and following behind.

CHAPTER 12

*T*he dank passageway looked, smelled, and felt like every Gothic nightmare I've ever had. The rock walls dripped with moisture, whispers of sound echoed from disconcerting directions, and our footsteps kicked up the scent of rotting fish. Mercifully, the smell abated as we proceeded up the tunnel. I could see in the flickering lantern light that the walls here were no longer comprised of rock but of earth, reinforced with lumber. My back ached from not being able to stand upright.

"Is it much farther?" I whispered.

The boy shook his head. We turned a corner, abruptly coming upon a plank door. It had once had a lock, long ago rusted and broken.

The door had warped over time. We had to tug hard to get it open. Once inside, I was finally able to stand upright.

"Whew. Any other lanterns in here?"

He shook his head. "None that I seen."

I took the light from him and shone it around. "How far under the inn does this space extend?"

He shrugged. "Dunno, miss."

Old, empty wooden crates lined the walls and a battered

workbench held a scattering of corks, broken glass, and a length of chain. I hefted the latter in my hand and shook it. Yes, that could have made the sound I had heard, though muffled. I shone the light behind the crates and pushed a stack away from the wall.

"Help me, will you?" I called. Between the two of us, we moved several stacks out of the way.

Behind the crates was a stout oak door with a new lock.

The boy sucked in a breath. "Lordy!"

Jack came over, sniffing avidly as far under the door as his snout could reach. Lucas and I pulled on the door, to no avail. The lock held fast. I moved the light closer. None of my picks would work on this one. How was I going to get in?

Lucas tried putting his eye to the gap in the hinges. "Ya think there's *treasure* in there?" His voice rose with excitement.

I suppressed a grimace, not inclined to involve the boy further. I affected an air of disinterest. "Probably not. It looks as if this place hasn't been used in years." I swung the lantern away from the new lock. "Shouldn't you be getting back to the stables? They might be missing you." I would return on my own once I had figured out how to unlock the door.

The boy gave a disgruntled sigh. "I guess so."

We pushed the crates against the door again and headed out of the tunnel. I counted paces as we went, trying to estimate how far under the inn the tunnel might extend. I noticed the hem of my striped silk had suffered a few smudges that would need Granny Aubry's special care.

We had just regained the path and parted ways—the boy heading to the stables and me to the dock below—when I noticed a man leaning against the dock railing, smoking his pipe, and watching me with narrowed eyes. I hoped I was too far away for him to determine exactly where I'd been.

As I approached, I recognized the deeply lined face and white push-broom mustache of Dr. Marsh. He lifted his hat in greeting.

"Is anyone ill?" I asked.

He smiled. "Not that I'm aware. Taggart has arranged a fishing excursion for the gentlemen and invited me along. I'm waiting for him to return with the ladies. They went out canoeing." He gestured with his pipe to some dots in the distance. "That'll be them now." Looking at me curiously, he asked, "How are you getting along, Madame? Seen any ghosts yet?"

I shrugged. Although I knew the man was a friend of Meyer's, he also seemed cozy with Captain Straub. I was not about to volunteer information or fuel suppositions that might reach Atwater's ears. "None so far."

He tapped his pipe against a tree trunk to knock out the ashes. "I heard something about a jewel going missing last night?"

I smiled to myself. The small-town gossip chain never fails. No doubt the laundress was a chatty sort. "It was merely mislaid and has since been recovered."

"Ah. Well, that is good news. Poor Jacob doesn't need any more trouble."

"I hardly think ghost stories are enough to scare away clientele."

"I wouldn't be so sure, Madame." Marsh kept his eye on the canoes as they approached. "A few years ago, I read a newspaper account of a speech Mr. Clemens gave. He said 'a truth is not hard to kill, and a lie told well is immortal.' Dashedly perceptive, that Clemens fellow. It happens all the time, does it not?"

Alas, I had no rejoinder. I had seen it myself. My estranged husband had told many a lie that seemed easier to believe than the truth.

The sounds of laughter, singing, and lively chatter soon drifted across the water. I could see the occupants more clearly now. Cassie shared a boat with Phillip Kendall and Amalie Joubert. I smiled. Cassie looked positively radiant, with a becoming flush to her cheeks and a sparkle in her eyes. The breeze ruffled strands of dark hair that had escaped her straw hat. The effect was soft, feminine, charming. She was attending to something Kendall was

79

saying, then threw her head back and laughed. From the gratified look on Kendall's face, I could see he enjoyed such devoted attention.

I suppressed a sigh. I hoped Cassie would not give her heart away.

"Something troubling you, Madame?" Marsh asked.

I recovered myself. "No, not at all." I hesitated. Marsh seemed privy to the local gossip. "What do you know about...Phillip Kendall?"

There was no way to make the inquiry sound casual. Marsh nodded knowingly as he watched the canoes glide toward the dock. "You are concerned for your friend? Understandable. She's a bit out of her league, if you will forgive me saying so."

I had considered that as well, though I had to bite off a retort nonetheless. "How so?" I asked instead.

"I've formed only a general impression of his character, you understand—a few dinner parties since his arrival two weeks ago and stories I hear from others...." He hesitated.

"And what is that impression?" I pressed.

He flushed and cleared his throat. "It is a delicate subject to bring up in feminine company, Madame."

"You mean he has an eye for the ladies?"

Marsh nodded. "Wealthy and famous ones in particular. I heard he and Miss Joubert once had an *affaire d'coeur.*"

After my eavesdropping in the rose garden last night, that was not exactly news. "You say he has been here two weeks?"

"Yes. He plans on staying the entire month, Meyer says."

I suddenly remembered the cufflink I had found in the room last inhabited by Lady Burton. "Any *affaires d'coeur* during his stay?"

His lips curled beneath his mustache. "That is hardly an appropriate topic of conversation with a lady. But I would warn your friend away from him, if I were you."

My gaze strayed to Kendall, now unfolding his long legs from the canoe and stepping up to the dock, gallantly helping the ladies alight. This was a complication I did not need.

Taggart jumped out of the last canoe and helped Misses Holloway and Barrington to the dock. He glanced at Marsh. "I'll be right back with the rods. The other gentlemen are waiting for us at the cove."

Cassie approached and tucked her arm through mine. "We had a wonderful time. I'm sorry you couldn't join us." She dropped her voice. "Did everything turn out all right? Meyer's look was black as thunder when I left."

"Yes, it's fine now," I murmured. I gave a quick nod as Kendall came up the path behind us. "Not joining the fishing party, Mr. Kendall?"

He chuckled. "Hardly. I fail to see the appeal of baiting a hook with something disagreeable, using it to catch something equally disagreeable, and eating it. I'm happy to profess ignorance as to where my food originates."

After years of hunting and shooting during my youth, I had ceased to be squeamish about such things. It was amusing to see a man behave so. Apparently, you can take the man out of the city, but not the city out of the man.

"You don't seem enthralled with rural life," I observed, falling into step with him. His long strides matched my own, although we both slowed for Cassie to catch up. "I'm curious as to why you would prolong your stay at the inn. You have been here a couple of weeks already, I understand."

He gave me a quick glance. "I needed a change of scene. The city in summertime can be quite oppressive."

"I'll say," Cassie chimed in, huffing to catch her breath.

I slowed my pace further. "How nice that you can take the time away from your business concerns. What is it you do, Mr. Kendall?"

He gave a little laugh. "I have stock interests in several companies—shipping, mostly—but don't have to bother with them much. I have a man who tends to that sort of thing." He waved a dismissive hand. "Let us talk of lighter matters. What is next on the schedule, ladies?"

Cassie fanned her flushed cheeks. "I could do with some lemonade."

"Excellent! We shall have it brought to the gazebo," Kendall said. "It's much cooler in the shade."

I looked behind me. Miss Joubert was coming up the walk, followed by the young ladies. "Would you like to join us for lemonade in the gazebo?" I called.

Squeals of delight met my invitation, though out of the corner of my eye I saw Cassie's frown.

Kendall's eyes lit up. "I shall make the arrangements." With a little bow, he turned and ran ahead.

"Why did you do that?" Cassie hissed, as soon as he was out of earshot. "This could have been my chance to get to know him better, without yammering females vying for his attention."

Exactly so. I sighed. "He's not quite the gentleman he seems, I am sorry to say. He has a reputation for...philandering." I wondered about other aspects of the man. Stock interests? Shipping? All conveniently vague. He'd changed the subject quickly. Of course, it was possible he assumed we ladies had no head for business matters. I have found that an annoyingly common assumption.

Cassie folded her arms and glared. "What nonsense. You know what I think? You are jealous. He's not interested in you, so you are keeping him away from me. I would not have believed it of you, Pen. I have given up so much for you. Why can you not allow *me* a bit of happiness?"

Before I could reply, she ran up the path after Kendall.

CHAPTER 13

J decided to forego the gazebo gathering and leave Cassie to flirt in peace. I wouldn't have been able to stop her anyway. My meddling seemed to have achieved the opposite effect.

It occurred to me that this was a rare opportunity to search Spencer Rayburn's room. He and the other men wouldn't be back from their fishing excursion for quite a while, and everyone else was either in the gazebo or down by the water. I would only have to keep an eye out for Mrs. Davis or a maid.

I pulled out my lockpicks and hurried up to the third-floor room directly over mine.

The hall was empty. First, I tested the door. Locked, as expected. I reached for my picks and soon had it open.

Rayburn was orderly in the extreme. Shoes lined up precisely in front of the armoire, cases stacked neatly in the corner, drawers occupied by folded shirts, collars, and bowties. I groped carefully between, under, and behind the piles. Nothing that shouldn't be there.

I went to the desk next. The odor of stale cigar was strongest here, although the ashtray had already been emptied. The desk drawers held several cigar cases. I checked them. Nothing but cigars. Atop the desk were pens and a neat stack of papers. I riffled through the sheets, glancing at the writing before restoring them to their place. Rayburn had been telling the truth. He was indeed writing a memoir. And badly, at that, but I wasn't here to judge the quality of his prose.

After going through the rest of his room and finding nothing more alarming than a shrunken head in a case—disturbing in a different way, but perhaps he'd brought it to impress the ladies—I slipped back out and locked his door. I checked my watch. Twenty minutes had gone by. I had time for one more room before any guests from the gazebo were likely to return.

I very much wanted to see Phillip Kendall's room. Like Rayburn, he had been a guest here last week, when the jewels disappeared. Perhaps he supplemented his business income with a little thieving on the side.

But which room was his? I would have to do it the hard way.

I'd gotten quite adept at the locks by the time I reached it, the fifth one down the hall from Rayburn's. I breathed a sigh of relief as I closed the door behind me and checked my watch.

Twenty-five minutes now. I would have to be quick. I cast my eye about the room. Where Rayburn was neat as a pin, Kendall was slovenly. Clothes were draped upon chair back and bed, shoes were shoved in a corner, loose change and other debris from pockets were scattered upon the dressing table. I picked through that first, plucking a decorative pin out of the jumble.

No, not a pin. A black enameled cufflink. I was sure it was the mate to the one I'd found yesterday, in the room that had formerly been Lady Burton's. I sighed and put it back. He and the lady must have had a dalliance. Had he seen fit to relieve her of her necklace as well as her virtue? If he was the thief I sought—entirely possible, and now a more likely candidate than Rayburn—how had he managed to steal the jewelry belonging to the Margeaux sisters? They had shared a room. There would have been no opportunity for a private dalliance there. Perhaps they were careless about locking their door when they went out.

My neck prickled with excitement. If he was the thief I sought, the jewels must *still be here.*

I continued my search in earnest, pulling out drawers, groping beneath the bed, opening the armoire and sifting through its contents. Silk ties, cashmere jacket, Egyptian cotton collars and cuffs…the man had expensive taste in clothing.

I was about to give up when I noticed the window seat, a feature my balcony room did not have. I lifted the lid. A stack of blankets occupied the storage space underneath. I pushed them aside, and my fingers felt a rough notch cut from the bottom panel. I pulled.

My heart beat faster as I extracted a worn leather pouch from the recess and opened it. I sucked in a breath.

No, not jewelry, but just as damning. A set of lockpicks, more extensive than my own.

I was so absorbed in my discovery that I had not attended to the passage of time or to the sound of footsteps in the corridor. By the time I heard the key rattling in the lock, it was too late. I froze, pouch in hand, as the door swung open.

Phillip Kendall stood in the doorway, eyes wide, white-knuckled hand still clenching the knob. "*You?* What the devil are you doing in my room?" He caught sight of the pouch and let out a sharp hiss. After looking over his shoulder and closing the door, he took the pouch from my hands.

Finally, I recovered my voice. "*You* are the jewel thief. Are you that desperate for funds? Or has this been your primary livelihood all along?" *Not shipping.*

He looked me up and down, the anger receding, replaced by an expression I couldn't quite fathom. "Sit down. Let us first address what you are doing in my room, shall we?"

I sat, trying to arrange my skirts so the bulge of my own lock-picks wouldn't show. "I apologize."

"I did not ask for an apology. I want to know who you are, why you are here, and"—he gestured to my skirt pocket—"why you carry a set of lockpicks."

I flushed. Drat the man. "Well, *you* obviously find them useful, so why not? One might ask you the same question."

"I asked first. Did you come here on the pretense of being a spirit medium, but in fact to steal from the wealthy guests here at the inn?"

"If that is my purpose, why am I here in your room?" I retorted. "I would have searched the Hollisters' room, or the Barringtons'."

"Who knows? Perhaps you have already been in there."

"Actually, I have, but not today." I groped in my pocket for—ah yes, there it was. The cufflink. I held it up. "You have been missing this, have you not? I found it in the room the Hollisters now occupy, which had been Lady Burton's room a week ago. It was under the bed."

Kendall paled.

"And there is the mate to it," I went on, nodding toward the dresser. "Did you bed Lady Burton first, Mr. Kendall, then slip away with her necklace after she was asleep? More enjoyable than employing your picks on the sly, but despicable nonetheless."

Kendall threw his head back and laughed.

I frowned. "I don't find this amusing."

"Your information is incomplete, Madame Cerise—is that really your name? It doesn't suit you. No matter. Lady Burton is eighty-five if she is a day and came to the inn to chaperone her great-grandnieces. Although she wasn't much of a chaperone. She spent most of her time dozing in the sunroom. I had no amorous intent toward her whatsoever. Or the young ladies." He blew out a breath. "I'm not a cradle-robber."

"Oh." Perhaps he was not quite the cad I'd originally thought. "So you were only stealing from her and lost your cufflink in the process?"

He raised an amused eyebrow. "*Only* stealing from her? You

possess an interesting set of principles, Madame." He grimaced. "What are you going to do?"

"That depends." An idea was beginning to form. "Do you still have the items you stole from Lady Burton and her great-grandnieces?"

His lip curled. "You didn't find those, did you?"

In an instant, I realized where they must be. "Of course not," I retorted. "I do not have access to the safe, Mr. Kendall."

I'd recalled Meyer's words. *One of the gentlemen lodgers is using it now.*

I had to admit, I was impressed by the man's imagination. It was a clever hiding place. Delightfully ironic, too.

Kendall's mouth hung open for a moment. "Who *are* you?"

"You are in no position to demand answers from *me*, sir." I stood.

He plucked an invisible speck of lint from his sleeve and affected an air of insouciance. "So, you are going to turn me in."

I bit my lip. I was about to cross a line, but my options were few. "No, I am not." I held up a hand as he was about to speak. "However, I have several conditions."

His eyes narrowed. "Conditions?"

"First, retrieve the jewels from the safe and give them to me. I will make sure they reach their rightful owners later. Second, make no further attempt to steal Miss Joubert's opal or the jewels of anyone else at the inn."

He shifted from one foot to the other. "Amalie was incredibly careless of the gem. Simply left it behind in her napkin."

"But you had regrets as soon as you took it, did you not? The disappearance of such a piece would attract a great deal of attention. So you put it back during the night."

"You knew it was me all along?"

I shrugged. I was not about to tell him of my earlier suspicions regarding Rayburn. "You made the mistake of putting Miss Joubert's necklace back in the Rose Room instead of somewhere out on the grounds. Only Mrs. Davis, Mr. Meyer, or one of the guests would have been able to do that. We had searched the room thoroughly that night, and the staff that lives in town had already left."

Kendall folded his arms. "You are astonishingly clear-minded for a woman."

The left-handed compliment hardly endeared him to me. I let it pass. "I have another condition. Distance yourself from Miss Leigh. Do it as kindly as you can." My voice grew subdued. "She has developed feelings for you."

He smiled. "I'm flattered. She is a charming woman. Done. Anything else?"

"I wish to borrow your picks, just for the night. Mine are inadequate for my purposes."

He hesitated, glancing down at the pouch in his hands. His long, thin fingers clenched protectively over the leather.

"I give you my word I shall take good care of them and return them to you tomorrow. I'm not interested in converting you to a model of good citizenship, Mr. Kendall. The decisions you make once you leave this inn are entirely your own affair."

He grinned as he passed them over. "I have never met a woman like you, Madame. What a shame we don't have the time to become better acquainted."

I flushed as I turned to leave. "Indeed."

CHAPTER 14

*T*he rest of the afternoon passed quietly at the inn. Guests read, napped, chatted, and visited the bathing hole. Cassie sulked in the library. She wasn't talking to me, and I was too restless to socialize with the others. I tried to read on a bench beside a charming fountain but found myself staring at the same paragraph for twenty minutes. All I could think of was employing Kendall's lockpicks on the hidden door of the cellar, and I couldn't attempt that until everyone had retired for the night.

I toured the grounds. Insects hummed in the sun-drenched fields. The air was humid and devoid of any breeze. More like our Chicago weather than a lakeside retreat, but Meyer had assured us such warm spells were short-lived.

After a time, I strolled along the rose garden paths and came upon the gardener. Though stooped with age—easily in his sixties —he reached for the blooms with nimble fingers. At his feet lay a large basket partly filled with roses.

He touched his hat brim, then returned to snipping stems.

"Are these for the table arrangements?" I asked.

He nodded. With a wide smile crinkling his tanned, craggy face, he gallantly presented me with a single red bloom.

I held it gingerly between the thorns as I breathed in the fragrance. "Thank you, Mr.—?"

"Zeke, miss." His voice was gravelly, as if he didn't have occasion to use it very often. "Jes' Zeke. My pleasure."

He squinted at the slant of the sun. "Gettin' late." He moved more quickly along the row.

"Do you need any help?" I offered. "I am rather at loose ends at the moment, and I do miss my garden."

He eyed me skeptically. "Do ya know how to cut a rose, miss? Ya can't just hack at it."

I took the shears and expertly snipped a stem.

His eyes brightened. "Ah, very good. I can see ya know your way around these beauties. I'd be much obliged for your help." He pointed to the next row. "We need another dozen o' the white ones, same length as the red. Jes' leave the basket on the table in the foyer. I'll be back right quick." He produced a pair of work gloves from his overalls and hurried away.

The roses were fragrant in the warmth of the afternoon. I threaded my gloved hands into the bushes, dodging thorns and fat bumblebees, seeking out the best, unblemished blooms. The sun was no longer directly overhead. A light breeze ruffled my hair. For a few blessed moments, my preoccupations fell away.

On my way back inside, I noticed the gardener walking away from an old stump near the road. The sun reflected off something shiny on its surface. He had left several coins behind but hadn't noticed.

"Zeke!" I called.

He changed direction and hurried towards me. "Finished already? Thank ya, miss. Much obliged." He took the basket, gloves, and shears.

I pointed to the stump. "I believe some coins fell out of your pocket."

He frowned. "Ah...yes, I see. Well, I'll jes' leave them there for the boy to find. It's a little game we play a'times." He tipped his cap and walked away.

For all his casual air, I knew the gardener was keeping an eye on me, so I strolled toward the gazebo. Once I was out of sight of the windows, I circled the house and slipped back to the stump. The coins were gone.

CHAPTER 15

*D*inner was to be a more formal affair tonight, so Cassie and I dressed in our best gowns. In the excitement of our preparations, my friend seemed to have forgiven my earlier interference.

"What do you think?" She held up two decorative hair combs. "The burgundy feathers or the marcasite?"

"The marcasite strikes me as more elegant and complements the jet beading on your gown."

"Do you think...Mr. Kendall will like it?" She blushed. "I know you don't approve of him, but once you come to know him, perhaps you'll change your mind."

I bit back the retort that I knew him all too well.

To be fair, at least he was proving to be a man of his word. The stolen jewelry was now in my possession, wrapped in a capacious kerchief and tucked away with the only two items that could give away my true identity—my logbook and picks. Kendall's picks were secreted there for the time being as well.

I weighed my words carefully. "My approval doesn't matter. But there is something else you should know. I overheard Mr. Kendall and Miss Joubert in the rose garden last night. There is a history between them, and I'm not sure that is over. You have seen how attentive he is around her." When Cassie dropped her eyes and fell silent, I added, "You know I only want your happiness? I do not wish to see you hurt."

She plucked at her skirt. "I know. However, I must judge what is best. I'm a grown woman."

I opened the top drawer to get my fan. "Fair enough. I—"

Wait. Something wasn't right.

My stockings and the other small items I kept in the drawer were slightly disarranged. I checked the other drawers and the armoire. Yes, someone had searched through my things.

Cassie's brow furrowed. "Pen, what is it?"

When had this happened? I'd laid out my dress and other items for tonight's dinner before heading outside to the fountain this afternoon. Both Cassie and I were out of our rooms for quite some time. We had locked our doors.

Who was responsible? One of the maids, indulging in idle curiosity? Mrs. Davis? The housekeeper had taken a distinct dislike to me.

I felt a chill. There was another possibility. Phillip Kendall, wanting to steal the jewels back. Perhaps I had not taken *all* of his picks.

"Pen," Cassie repeated. "What is wrong?"

"Have your belongings been searched?" I asked.

She sucked in a breath and ran back to her room.

I checked my hiding place, in the gap between the bottom drawer and the back of the bureau. Everything was there—jewels, both sets of picks, logbook. The virtually invisible blond hairs I had draped across the book were undisturbed. I let out a breath and restored the drawer.

Cassie returned. "Everything in my room looks as it should. I don't think it was searched." She frowned. "Are you all right? You look a bit pale."

I straightened up and smoothed my skirt with clammy hands.

"I'll be fine. Shall we go down?" I carefully locked the door behind us.

It had not yet gone to dusk, but every candle and lamp was burning as we entered the dining room. The effect was merry and welcoming. And growing warmer by the minute. Thank heaven I'd selected a sleeveless gown. Of course, it was eight years old and had more flounces than was currently fashionable, but I was fond of the deep coral faille skirt and pearl-embellished bodice. My hair was done up in its usual coronet braid, with the pearl comb in the crown. I had to admit my vanity was gratified by the admiring looks of the gentlemen as they stood at our approach. *Frailty, thy name is woman.*

The other female guests, not to be outdone for male attention, had enough diamonds, sapphires, and other precious stones between them to finance my household expenses for the next five years. Kendall would be sorely pressed to keep his promise.

Mrs. Davis was joining us tonight. She was becomingly attired in a turquoise satin evening dress with a high neck and simple quarter train. Her aspect seemed softer, more feminine, as if she had shed her strict, authoritarian demeanor along with her uniform. Still, I never saw her smile.

Once we were gathered around the long dining table, Meyer introduced the local guests: Judge Knox, Dr. Marsh, Mrs. Becham, and Mr. Atwater. The latter had been at my request. I wasn't sure Meyer's rival would accept the invitation, but in a town of this size, one must keep up the pretense of joviality. *One may smile, and smile, and be a villain,* if I remembered my *Hamlet* correctly.

The Barringtons and Holloways were seated in the center grouping of chairs, having the advantage—or burden—of engaging in cross-conversations. I sat at the left end between Atwater and Kendall, with Miss Joubert on Kendall's other side and Cassie across from us, Dr. Marsh and Rayburn on either side of her. I was grateful that Meyer had arranged for me to sit beside

Atwater, but I wished Cassie were not so close to Kendall. I hoped Kendall would keep that promise as well.

The evening passed pleasantly, although Lionel Atwater was so engrossed in conversing with Mrs. Becham seated across from us that I had little opportunity to strike up a conversation with Meyer's business rival. I was obliged to converse instead with Rayburn, all the while watching the smile on Cassie's face grow stiffer and more pained as the meal went on. Kendall kept his attention focused upon Miss Joubert, Rayburn, and myself, with only the occasional polite acknowledgment of Cassie's presence. Perhaps I should not have stepped in.

No. Kendall was a thief and not at all the man for Cassie. Although he was not guilty of seducing Lady Burton, he had an easy way with women that the ladies in question would do well to guard against. He would have only brought grief to my friend.

"Madame Cerise?" A lilting voice interrupted my thoughts.

"Hmm? Ah yes, Miss Joubert, you have a question?"

The lady leaned past Kendall to make eye contact. "You mentioned a séance. Will you be conducting one tonight?"

I felt Atwater stiffen beside me. Was he nervous about spirits or guilty because he was the cause of the ghostly mischief?

"Not tonight," I said. "I hope to conduct a session tomorrow, after dark, when the spirits are most propitious." I glanced over at Meyer, who had been attending the conversation. "If that suits our host, of course." I held my breath. Would Meyer go along with the scheme?

He gave me a long look, then nodded.

Atwater let out a derisive snort. "You'll get nothing but thrill-seekers staying here with that nonsense, Jacob."

Meyer reddened but held his ground. "On the contrary, I think it will settle the ghost question once and for all." He locked eyes with me.

I smiled. "Indeed. And of course, everyone here is invited."

Mrs. Becham, sitting beside Meyer, leaned forward eagerly. "A *séance,"* she breathed. "How exciting! Do you not think so, Mrs. Davis?"

Hannah Davis folded her arms and glared in my direction. "*Hmph.* As long as you do not make another mess for me to clean up."

So much for her softened, feminine side. I inclined my head in acknowledgment.

Mrs. Becham frowned. "Tomorrow night, you say? That could be a problem."

"Why?" Cassie asked.

"Granny Aubry's knee has been acting up something awful today." Mrs. Becham sat back and said nothing more, as if that were sufficient explanation. Given the nods by the locals around the table, it apparently was.

Amalie Joubert's brows knit together. "And what, pray, does Granny's knee have to do with having a séance on Thursday?"

"The old lady's rheumatics are considered a reliable indicator of impending storms," Dr. Marsh said. "I cannot explain it scientifically, of course, but I must admit we've found her knee to be quite accurate."

"But there was not a cloud in the sky today," Cassie protested. "And the lake has been perfectly calm."

"Nevertheless, Granny's knee has never been wrong, in the thirty years that I've lived here," Marsh said. "Mark my words, tomorrow the waters will get choppy and the wind will start picking up." He looked over at Mrs. Becham. "She didn't send for me, though, so it cannot be hurting too badly. Perhaps it won't be much of a storm."

"The weather may hold off until after the séance," I suggested. "I hope you all will come."

We ladies retired to the Rose Room shortly after. Not wanting to incur Mrs. Davis's wrath, I read palms instead of tea leaves. A much less messy endeavor, to be sure. I was gratified to see that Miss Joubert's opal was securely around her neck the entire time.

After the gentlemen joined us and the coffee was served, I managed to find a place beside Atwater. I still wanted to learn more about the man.

Lionel Atwater helped me into my chair before re-seating himself. He pointed to the coffeepot. "Shall I freshen your cup, Madame?"

I nodded. "Are you a native to the area, Mr. Atwater, or a transplant like Mr. Meyer?"

He smiled. "I spent my entire life in these parts. Wonderful place, though you would hardly recognize it from its earlier days. The rail line didn't come through here until ten years ago. Once I saw how it was opening up the area, I built Cedar Lodge. I knew it would be a sound investment."

I inclined my head discreetly toward Meyer, who was helping Mrs. Davis set up card tables at the far end of the room. "Were you distressed when the competition moved in?"

Atwater hid a smirk behind his cup and took a sip before answering. "Not to be disrespectful of Meyer's little establishment here, but it is hardly *competition*. Cedar Lodge is much larger and offers all the latest amenities—private baths, steam heat in the cooler months, tennis courts, a greenhouse...we even have our own bakery."

"It sounds charming. I shall have to visit it sometime."

Atwater nodded. "Simply say the word, Madame. It would be my pleasure to show you around."

I returned to the subject at hand. "You do know about Meyer's expansion project? The building and grounds here are extensive. There is great potential. He may be a true competitor yet."

Atwater smiled and lifted his cup in mock salute. "*Potential* doesn't put money in one's pocket. Time will tell, Madame."

CHAPTER 16

*A*fter a long evening of cards, coaches took the locals home and the inn's guests retired for the night. I said good night to Cassie, changed into quiet slippers and a dark dress with deep pockets—packed expressly for the purposes of nighttime reconnoitering—and waited.

Finally, the noises of the house quieted. I stuffed a book of matches and Kendall's lockpicks in my pockets and wrapped myself in a shawl against the night chill.

A single lamp in the deep window casement offered modest illumination as I crept along the upper corridor. Just as I approached the stairs, I froze. Footsteps. I strained to find the source, breathing a sigh when I heard them again, overhead. Rayburn's room.

I waited. When it became obvious he was simply pacing, I continued down the stairs and outside. I hurried toward the gardener's shed, hoping the lantern I'd seen hanging there yesterday was still in its place.

Yes, there it was. Perfect. I would have to wait until I was out of sight of the windows to light it. With both hands on the lantern

—the metal handle squeaked terribly—I crept over to the padlocked root cellar hatch beside the kitchen door.

Between the low light and the unfamiliar picks—Kendall did not keep his set organized by size or any other system that I could determine—it took me some time to find the proper tool to open the lock. I finally managed it and eased open the doors just enough to slip inside. I lit the lantern, then made sure the door was back in place. Unless one looked carefully and saw the padlock was off, it should be virtually unnoticeable from the outside.

It was a steep, dirt slope to the now-empty vegetable bins against the back wall. The walls were shored with lumber that had blackened with age. The space was so low and cramped that I was obliged to keep to a crouched posture as I made my way down. The sensation of an airless tomb made my nape prickle with unease.

I swung my light toward the sounds of scurrying. A pair of eyes flashed briefly.

Ugh. I hate rats.

I explored the space thoroughly nonetheless, looking for another door that led back to the room and the tunnel Lucas had shown me. My search turned up nothing. I had wondered if the room with the new lock upon it would have its exit here. It had been difficult to tell by counting paces. Unfortunately, I would have to access it by way of the tunnel at the lakeshore.

As I emerged from the root cellar hatch, I heard a rustling sound. My heart pounding, I shuttered my lantern and slipped behind a lattice of climbing roses. A stiff breeze had picked up. I huddled into my shawl. Perhaps there was something to Granny's trick knee after all.

After several minutes of hearing nothing unusual, I turned up my lantern and hurried down the path to the lake. It was going to be a challenge to find the entrance in the dark.

Snuffling noises a few feet ahead made me jump. It was Jack, tail wagging. He looked at me expectantly, cocking his head to one side.

I let out a breath. "So, it was you that I heard. No treats for you, naughty dog. You scared me to death."

The beagle jumped up to lick my hand, then trotted next to me as I followed the path towards the soft sounds of water lapping the shore. I veered off the path at what I hoped was the correct place. My former nervousness fell away. Perhaps it was having the dog by my side, small as he was.

"Where's the tunnel, boy?" I asked him.

I felt a bit silly, but as if he understood me, Jack bounded ahead. I followed him until a familiar pile of boulders came into view. At the cave entrance, I stopped to catch my breath and patted him on the head. "All right, then, you've redeemed yourself. We'll get you a nice, big stick to play with once we're done."

I opened the lantern shutter fully, and we went in.

Although I had the benefit of experience, the tunnel felt even more eerie and sinister in the blackness of night. The sounds were magnified, the odors more intense. The hound kept his nose to the ground and forged ahead. When we reached the chamber, I wasted no time pulling away the stacked crates that concealed the door to the room beyond. The lantern was sputtering in an alarming fashion, its fuel running low. I would have to hurry.

I felt both hot and chilled at the same time in the damp air, perspiration trickling down my forehead and my back. I finally found the right pick but struggled to grip it between sweaty palms. With no hands free, I kept the lantern light fixed upon the lock by clenching the handle with my teeth. Not in the Pinkerton manual, but one must be inventive.

At last, the lock released, and I stepped inside. This room was higher than the other, with the inn's sub-flooring comprising part of the ceiling. Wooden pallets had been positioned atop the packed earth to form an improvised floor.

The dog let out a low growl even before I heard the footsteps

K.B. OWEN

approach. I snuffed the lantern, grabbed the dog, and pressed against the wall behind the door. I hoped Jack had more of a killer instinct than his happy-go-lucky personality had shown thus far.

CHAPTER 17

The light of another lantern preceded the man. I glimpsed long, pale, manicured fingers grasping the handle. I relaxed my grip on the dog. I recognized those fingers.

Phillip Kendall whipped around as I stepped calmly into the pool of light. The dog jumped up, putting his front paws up on Kendall's trousers, tail wagging, whining for attention.

So much for killer instinct.

Kendall blew out a breath. "Ah, I thought I'd find you here."

"Have you been following me all the while?" I didn't trouble to keep the irritation from my voice.

He scratched the dog behind an ear. "I have been curious about you, Madame. You are a walking set of contradictions. A spirit medium who carries a set of picks and employs them with abandon, knows the names and rooms of guests who had jewelry stolen a week before her arrival, extracts a promise from a confirmed thief that he will not steal any more jewels during the remainder of the week and will, in fact, relinquish the ones already stolen…and then borrows the tools of the aforementioned thief for some vague purpose? I was convinced you were no mere ghost hunter, if you were even that."

I winced. In my zeal to learn the secrets of Schroon Lake Inn, I had been careless of my cover.

"I would have said you are a thief yourself, who had successfully blackmailed me out of my own plunder," he went on. "However"—my heart clenched as he pulled a familiar-looking book out of his pocket—"I searched your room after you left and found this."

My logbook.

I most definitely had *not* confiscated all of his picks. The cheek of the man. I folded my arms and glared. "And I suppose you took back the jewels I'd secreted in the same hiding place?"

He raised an eyebrow. "I am insulted, Madame. They are exactly where you left them. But the book…ah, this is the real treasure." He tapped a page. "This entry is my particular favorite: 'Phillip Kendall's thieving is born of long practice and skill. I have no doubt he has been stealing valuables from the upper crust of society for quite some time without detection. His victims are women readily susceptible to his questionable charms. While not exactly a desperate character, caution is warranted.'"

I sighed. My hiding place had not fooled him in the least. Which made me wonder….

"Was tonight the only time you had searched my room?" I asked.

He looked up with narrowed eyes. "Yes, it was my first opportunity since our fascinating conversation in my room this afternoon. Why?"

Surprisingly, I believed him. "When I dressed for dinner, I discovered my things had been disturbed."

He frowned. "It appears someone else is wondering about you, Madame."

The conclusion was inescapable. I held out my hand for the book. "If you please."

He handed it over. "Although I doubt that, whoever it is, imagines you are a *lady* detective." He shook his head. "Extraordinary. But it explains a great deal."

His eyes were dark and inscrutable in the flickering light. I felt a chill. Now that he knew what I was, to what lengths would he go in order to avoid the law?

He turned away, shining his light on the walls. The dog wandered over to a corner and occupied himself with sniffing along the floor.

I let out a breath. For just a moment, I had mistrusted my earlier instincts about the man.

As the fuel in my own lantern was too low to re-light it, I followed Kendall as he explored the chamber. It was my first good look at the space. Two rows of old empty barrels lined the back wall. A shiny-new handcart was propped in a corner, and pieces of copper coil lay scattered upon a long table.

"What is all this?" I asked.

Kendall stuck his head in a barrel and pulled it out, grimacing. "A distillery operation, I'd say. Smells like cheap rum was in this one."

Moonshiners. Things were beginning to make sense. "When? As recently as this past spring, perhaps?"

He nodded as he looked around the room. "It looks to be a mix of old"—he pointed to the barrels—"and new"—he nodded towards the handcart. "It's an ideal place for it. No one would discover them here."

"Certainly when the inn lay abandoned for a decade. However, they must have feared discovery when Meyer moved in. First, they tried sabotaging his equipment. When that didn't work, I believe they attempted to continue their activities for a time, late at night, hoping that whatever sounds were heard"—I pointed to the subfloor above us—"would be attributed to a ghost. No doubt they were reluctant to move their operation elsewhere. That had to be quite an undertaking."

"Around these remote parts, selling moonshine isn't big business," Kendall said, opening another barrel and tentatively sniffing. "Usually it's a farmer with a small still in his barn, turning blackstrap molasses into rum and selling bottles to the locals." He wrinkled his nose. "Or fruit mash into cheap apple brandy." He put the lid back on.

I sighed. "I would say our gardener is a regular customer." Zeke's odd behavior—furtively placing something under the hedge, leaving coins behind on the stump, his preoccupation with the time—it all made sense. He was paying for his liquor at pre-arranged intervals. And the cart driving down the road at dusk the other evening—had that been a delivery?

Even so, I was willing to bet there was more to this than supplying illicit rum to the locals. "This seems a larger operation."

"What do you mean?"

"We are situated right on the lake. Steamers such as the *Galene* make frequent stops at the nearby dock. It wouldn't be difficult for someone like Captain Traub to take on crates of bottled moonshine and deliver them to points along Schroon Lake. And beyond, if we consider the rail line. That extends their reach."

Kendall let out a low whistle. "You may be right."

I noticed a huddle of white beneath the worktable. Rags? I picked up the cloth and spread it out. White powder came loose and drifted to the ground.

"What's that?" Kendall asked, shining the light.

I held it up against him. It was long enough to go over his head and still trail upon the ground. "I'd say we found our ghost. Someone has been play-acting." Perhaps it had been a last-ditch effort to avoid moving the distillery. It was a miscalculation on their part, however, as it made Meyer more determined than ever to go to William Pinkerton to get to the bottom of the ghost business.

Kendall brushed the white powder—probably flour—from his jacket. "Rayburn told me someone had seen a ghost. It happened just before I got here. He said the lady's shrieks woke the entire establishment." He chuckled.

The dog's whine got our attention. I groaned at the sight of a pallet having been up-ended and a very large mound of earth now piled beside a fresh hole. "Jack! Bad boy. You can't go digging here."

He let out a sharp *yip*, and we came over for a closer look. My heart clenched when I saw what he had unearthed.

Kendall sucked in a breath. "Is that what I think it is?" He pointed to the long, pale object poking through the dirt.

I crouched down and brushed more of the dirt away. My heart pounded in my throat. "Yes. It's a bone." I scooped up more dirt. "And look, here are more."

"An animal?" His voice quavered.

I silently shook my head. Schroon Lake Inn had given up its final secret. I was sure we had found the missing proprietor, Artie Willis.

CHAPTER 18

*T*he dog abruptly lifted its head, cocking its ears toward the door. Someone was coming. I shoved the pick into Kendall's hand. "Lock the door," I whispered. My hands were shaking too badly to do it myself.

One benefit of working with a thief is that he tends to act first and ask questions later. Kendall soon had the lock secured and the lantern shuttered. We huddled with the dog in a corner behind the worktable, as the heavy tread of several men approached. A bright light came from beneath the door.

The latch jiggled, followed by a sharp oath.

"Told yer it'd be locked."

"Well, then, pass me the key, Mr. Smarty."

"Clive has it."

"Naw. I thought *you* had it!"

I didn't recognize any of the voices. Knowing they couldn't get in, I began to relax, and in the process realized that Kendall was protectively shielding me with his body. The man had a touch of the gallant about him that was endearing.

It was also rather disconcerting, however, as I became aware of the warmth of his torso pressed against me and his smooth, strong hands clasping mine to still their trembling. I tried to quiet my breathing and slow the pounding of my heart as I pulled my hands away. It had been years since I'd been this physically close to an attractive man. I had forgotten how it felt.

The quarrel on the other side of the door continued. "He ain't gonna be happy if we don' come back with the cart. You already gummed up the works by not bringing it back with ya in the first place. And look here!" The voice grew shrill with anxiety. "You didn't even hide the door like yer supposed to! I'm sick o' tellin' ya that."

"I swear, I did!" the other man protested.

I heard a snort. "Yeah, right. Go back an' get the key, you numskull. We'll wait for you by the entrance. This place gives me the willies."

Their voices faded as they moved back down the tunnel. Kendall stood, dusted off his trousers, and helped me up. "I wouldn't recommend waiting around for them to return."

"We cannot leave the way we came," I pointed out. "You heard them. They'll be waiting at the end of the tunnel." I opened the lantern shutter wide and held it high above our heads, along the subflooring of the inn.

"What are you doing?"

"Looking for another way out. The shrieking lady we were just talking about? Meyer put Miss Leigh and me in those rooms. I didn't see any sort of opening or panel in my room, but I had not checked hers yet." I was reproving myself for that oversight.

"You mean some sort of secret passage?" He frowned. "That sounds like something out of a penny dread—" He broke off as I found a well-concealed handhold in what I was willing to bet was a trap door.

I struggled to pull it down. "Your assistance would be most welcome, Mr. Kendall." He couldn't see my smirk in the dim light. Penny dreadful, indeed.

Although the panel was heavy, it opened quietly on well-oiled hinges. He boosted me through the gap and passed me the lantern. The space was not as dusty as I'd expected. Ladder-style footholds were anchored to the inside back wall of the inn, taking advantage of a little extra depth created by the recessed window seat of the dining room above and stretching beyond the first floor. Up to Cassie's room, most likely. The lantern didn't illuminate the space that far. Well, we would find out where it ended. We certainly couldn't stay here.

I wedged the lantern in a recess just above my shoulder. "Give me the dog."

"Just a moment." Kendall disappeared from view for a few minutes. I heard scraping noises, and then he returned.

He passed up the beagle, who wriggled excitedly in my arms and started licking my cheek. "What were you doing?" I whispered.

"I re-covered the bones as best as I could and moved the pallet back in place. We don't want them to see that, do we?"

"Good thinking." With one arm firmly around the dog, I stretched out a hand to help Kendall, but he waved it aside. He easily hoisted himself up.

I moved up a step to give him room. "You are a second-story man as well, I take it."

He cleared his throat awkwardly as he closed the hatch behind us.

I passed him the dog, then retrieved the lantern. "Let's go."

Our progress was slow. I tested each step before putting my full weight upon it, which turned out to be a wise precaution. One came away from its anchoring, and several others wobbled in place. The passageway was even more of a squeeze for the broad-shouldered Kendall. I imagined his fine jacket was ruined.

It was obvious the passage had been built well before Jacob Meyer's time. Artie Willis's doing, no doubt. But to what end? It was too steep and narrow to move moonshine equipment. Perhaps it was a bolt-hole, a place to hide should the room at the end of the tunnel be raided by the authorities. It was certainly proving useful for Kendall and me.

Had Willis been the ringleader of the operation or merely a willing participant? Had an associate killed him in a falling out? But then, why bury the body in the very place where they made the illicit brew? I was missing something here.

The innkeeper died ten years ago. The men on the other side of the door sounded too young for Willis's time and too scatter-brained to be running the show.

He ain't gonna be happy if we don' come back with the cart.

They feared the man in charge. Who was he? I bit my lip as I climbed and considered the possibilities. Josh Taggart was on the young side, but he was still a possibility. Zeke the gardener seemed more interested in taking custom than providing it. The local men at last night's dinner—Judge Knox, Dr. Marsh, Lionel Atwater—each had lived in the area ten years at least. I hesitated, my foot on the last step. Captain Traub. Yes, he was another prospect. An idea was beginning to form, a way to flush out the murderer. I was going to need help to make it work.

"Why have you stopped? Do you see a door?" Kendall's whis-pered voice interrupted my thoughts.

I gestured with the lantern. "There's a crack of light just ahead."

The panel was latched on this side. Probably why Meyer had not found it, and I would not have, either. The passage was intended as a one-way escape *from* the tunnel. After pushing the panel away, I batted at a faceful of dusty curtains. It was, indeed, Cassie's bedroom. I had just turned to relieve Kendall of the dog when I heard a shriek behind me.

"*Shh*, Cassie, it's me," I hissed, whipping around.

She brought the candle closer and gaped. I knew I must be a sight, covered in dirt and dust, my coronet undone in a fraying braid down my back. Her eyes widened when the dog jumped up on her bed and promptly went to sleep. I could hardly blame the pup. It had been a rough night.

Cassie stifled another shriek when a sheepish Phillip Kendall crawled out.

"What in the *Sam Hill* is going on here?" she cried. That was as close as my proper friend ever came to cursing.

I made a *shush*ing gesture and pointed to my room. "We should talk in there." I glanced uneasily at Kendall.

He nodded. "They might hear us." He closed the panel as much as he could, but without being able to secure it from this side, it hung open a crack.

Cassie dropped her voice. "*Who* might hear us?" She hastily put on her dressing gown and cinched it around her waist. Even in the dim light, I could see her blush. Kendall had discreetly turned his head.

Once we were in my room and had closed the connecting door, I explained to Cassie what had happened. Kendall arched an eyebrow over my omission of his lockpicks and profession, but I could tell he was grateful. I was going to need all of the goodwill I could muster.

Cassie sucked in a sharp breath when I got to the part about finding the body. "What are we going to do?"

"Why, catch the killer, of course," I said, more confidently than I felt. "Remember, the spirits see all and know all. That is our advantage."

Kendall snorted, but he and Cassie listened intently as I explained my plan.

Kendall's grin grew wider by the minute. "I must say, the past twelve hours have proved far more interesting than any time in recent memory."

I made a face at him. "For you, that is saying a great deal."

He threw back his head and laughed. Cassie gave us a puzzled look.

I got up to escort him to the door. "We should all get some sleep."

He shook his head. "I want the two of you to spend the night here. I will take Miss Leigh's room and keep watch, just in case our friends down below get suspicious and decide to come up. They may notice the grave has been disturbed."

Cassie paled. "Do you really think that could happen, Mr. Kendall?"

He shrugged. "It is best to be safe." He opened the connecting door. "Lock this behind me."

I was touched by his protectiveness. "No heroics," I warned. "If you hear anything, call out."

He smiled and waved toward the dog, snoring softly on Cassie's bed. "Don't worry. Jack will protect me."

CHAPTER 19

J didn't think I could possibly sleep, but whether it was the reassurance of Kendall keeping watch in the next room or the profound exhaustion that permeated every bone in my body, I fell into a dreamless sleep and didn't wake until an overcast, pale-dawn light started to seep through the curtains.

In the next room, floorboards creaked beneath a light tread. Kendall was up.

Moving carefully so as not to wake Cassie, I slipped out of bed and found my robe. I tapped quietly on the connecting door.

Kendall looked much the worse for wear—dark hair tousled, bearded shadow on his chin, dark smudges below his eyes, shirt rumpled. He was in his shirtsleeves, his dirty jacket slung over his arm. Still, he abounded with good spirits and gave me a ready smile. "Good morning, Madame," he murmured. "Nothing to report. All was well."

I breathed a sigh. Our presence in the cellar had not been detected. "You should get some sleep."

Jack, still on Cassie's bed, jumped down at the sound of our voices.

"I'll let him out," Kendall said, his hand on the knob.

"Thank you again for your help last night."

He grinned. "It has been my pleasure. I look forward to this evening." He cracked the door, listened, then slipped out.

I was just about to return to my room when I heard the voice of Miss Joubert calling from down the hall.

"Phillip! Whatever are you doing in Miss Leigh's room at this hour?"

Oh, no. I put my ear to the door, holding my breath.

"Keep your voice down, Amalie. You'll wake everyone."

She dropped her voice, though not her aggrieved air. "Oh, so we cannot disturb your paramour, is that it?"

Kendall's laugh was soft. "One hardly brings a *dog* to an assignation, my dear." A short bark accompanied the comment.

"Oh!"

"I'm afraid I cannot elaborate further. You will have to trust me...."

Their voices moved away, and I heard nothing more. I was tempted to intervene, but I had no idea what I could possibly say that would not make it worse. I didn't worry about Kendall giving us away. He knew the importance of keeping our plans a secret. However, without a satisfactory answer for Miss Joubert, I had no doubt there would be further trouble from that quarter today.

I was dressed and ready to head to breakfast by the time Cassie awoke. After warning her about Kendall being caught *in flagrante* outside her door—she took the news much better than I expected —I took the kerchief of jewels from their hiding place, stuffed them in my pocket, and hurried downstairs to speak with Meyer.

He escorted me to his office and closed the door.

"I've made progress in the case, Mr. Meyer, but I must warn you that some aspects are rather...distressing."

Meyer tucked his plump chin to his chest and sighed.

"Regarding the ghostly noises—"

"—I am more concerned with the jewel thefts," Meyer interrupted impatiently.

His mouth gaped as I pulled the handkerchief of jewels from my pocket and passed it over.

"Wh-where did you find them?" he asked finally.

"In a hidden room, beneath this building."

Some might take exception to my omission of Kendall's guilt. However, he had proved a loyal ally and would be of little use to me tonight if he were on his way to a holding cell. I would, of course, make a full report to Mr. Pinkerton when I returned to Chicago. He could decide what to do from there.

Meyer frowned in confusion. "The root cellar?"

"No, no, there's a tunnel from the lakeshore that leads to a pair of rooms just beneath the dining room of the inn. The entrance is well concealed. I think the original proprietor, Artie Willis, built it. As far as I can tell, the innermost underground chamber abuts the root cellar but doesn't connect to it. "

He sighed. "A tunnel...all this time...."

"I can show you, if you like."

"Later, perhaps." He turned the jewels over in his hands. "Who stole these, and why leave them behind?"

I shrugged. "It's hard to say, but I'm confident that you won't have to worry about future thefts, particularly once you nail shut the panel I found in Miss Leigh's room. That is the only other means of access from the underground rooms."

His mouth formed a silent *o* before he recovered his voice. "So there *is* a passageway? And the ghost—"

"—was most definitely a mortal being. I found a costume of sorts in the chamber below. Someone masqueraded as a ghost to frighten your guests."

Meyer gave a grunt. "Atwater."

"That is a safe assumption. He—or a confederate—dressed in the rags and entered the room through the access panel."

"Access panel? We searched for just such a thing," he protested.

"It was latched from the other side. You would not have been able to open it or even see that anything was out of order. It blends in with the other decorative beadboard panels. Willis built that, too."

He laced his fingers over his stomach with a sigh. "How did Atwater know about the underground rooms or passageway? And why go to so much trouble to drive me out? Does he really see me as such a threat to his business?"

"I suspect he's protecting another asset besides his lodge."

Meyer's eyes narrowed in the pudgy folds of his face. "Go on."

"The mysterious noises were not an attempt to scare your guests away, although I'm sure Atwater did his best to use them to that effect. They were the result of moonshiners."

"Moonshiners!" he exclaimed.

I got up and checked the door. The hallway was empty, thank goodness. "A bit more quietly, if you please." I closed the door. "Remember, the inn sat empty for ten years before you moved in. It was the ideal place for illicit activity, being so close to the lake as well as to the main road. Your arrival changed all that. That is why they first tried discouraging you by sabotaging your equipment and frightening your guests. When you continued in spite of it, they realized they could not proceed with business as usual because of the way the sound carries up the walls. They had to make other arrangements. I've seen evidence that they recently dismantled their equipment and relocated. That's why the ghostly noises grew worse for a time, then subsided."

Meyer sighed. "I suppose that makes sense. But why do you think Atwater is involved in making moonshine?"

"Whoever masqueraded as the ghost two weeks ago would have had to pass through the heart of the moonshine operation to access the passageway up to the Elk Suite. If you believe that person to be Atwater or a confederate of his, then he must be aware of the operation. I think he's in charge of it, in fact."

Meyer gave me a skeptical look.

I ticked off the list on my fingers. "If we assume that Willis himself was the original mastermind of the operation, back in the day—it's hard to imagine the rooms I saw being built without his knowledge—what happened after he disappeared? Who else knew the rooms and equipment were there? A partner in the original scheme makes the most sense. The tunnel is well concealed, and its existence is not common knowledge. Atwater is native to the area and was here during Willis's time—"

"—as are many locals," Meyer interrupted. "Our town doctor, Judge Knox, Captain Traub, even the Widow Becham. I don't care for Atwater, but we mustn't make assumptions out of hand."

"Indeed, we must not," I agreed, "and this is for your ears alone. However, have you ever wondered how Atwater financed the construction of Cedar Lodge? The expense must have been enormous. I cannot imagine the upkeep of such a place is cheap, either."

Meyer shrugged. "We should let the authorities take over now. You have fulfilled your task." His face softened. "For which I am grateful."

I suppressed a sigh. "Unfortunately, there is an additional complication." I told him about the grave.

He groaned. "I'll never have another guest again. The notoriety!"

"It will pass. At least Willis's relations will finally know the truth."

"So he did not run off," Meyer mused aloud, "and the grave has been there all this time." He heaved himself out of his chair. "I assume you wish me to send a cable to Chestertown's sheriff? He's the closest."

I shook my head. "Not yet. I'm hoping to trick the murderer into revealing himself tonight."

"After all these years? You have been reading too much sensation fiction, young lady. Why should we attempt such nonsense?"

"Because if you hand over a ten-year-old murder case to an out-of-town sheriff to investigate, you may never know who the killer is," I retorted. "In a place of this size, you would be socializing with the guilty man on a regular basis, always wondering, always suspicious."

Meyer rubbed a hand over his face. I waited.

He let out a deep breath. "What do you want me to do?"

"Take your cues from me tonight, during the séance. We will seek to create anxiety in the killer's mind. But first, I want you to extend an invitation to Captain Traub to attend."

"Traub? You think he did it?" Meyer asked incredulously.

"I don't know if he killed Willis, but who better than a steamer captain to be in on a scheme to smuggle moonshine, whether it was back in Willis's time or now? That may be another reason why he was willing to circulate ghost stories about your establishment. If he's not the murderer, he may know who is."

Meyer looked out the window, which rattled as a stiff breeze came up. Weak sunlight barely seeped through the cloud cover. "If Granny Aubry's knee is right, the weather may be too poor for any of the locals to attend."

I grimaced. "We'll see."

CHAPTER 20

*M*eyer went off to stow the jewels in the safe—of course, he couldn't know they had been there all along—until he could return them to their rightful owners. I joined Cassie at the breakfast buffet.

"Everything all right?" I murmured, reaching for a plate. Cassie gave a quick nod, her gaze focused upon spooning marmalade on her toast, but I could see the flush on her neck and cheeks.

One glance over my shoulder was enough to see that Miss Joubert had already spread the news about Kendall sneaking out of Cassie's room. Mrs. Barrington and Mrs. Hollister were huddled beside the singer, glaring in our direction.

"Let's take the table by the window." I led Cassie over and positioned her with her back to the harpies. "I'm sorry to have embroiled you in this," I added in a low voice.

Cassie shrugged. "I must admit to being flattered at first, that others would consider me the object of Mr. Kendall's attentions. But now I feel distinctly uncomfortable."

"The full story cannot be told until after the séance. Then we can straighten out the misunderstanding."

Cassie tossed her head defiantly. "It doesn't matter. We will never see these people again."

I smiled. It was good to see her plucky side. "Remember, I'll need your help tonight. It would be wise to complain of an indisposition before dinner and have a tray sent up. Then your absence at the séance will not be remarked upon."

She brightened. "Have you rigged the table?" she whispered.

I shook my head. "We are expecting too many people. A small one will no longer suffice, and something larger would be too heavy."

"Which of Madame Violette's items am I to use?"

"We'll keep it simple. Just some rapping and the bell. And ring it faintly, so that it seems muffled. I'll have the other one under glass on the table."

"I'll be in the cabinet in the Rose Room then, as planned?" She leaned forward, eyes wide with excitement.

"Actually, I'm moving the séance to the dining room. You'll be in the hidden passage behind the window seat. You should still be able to hear and cannot possibly be discovered."

Cassie's brows drew together in a worried frown.

"It is no more dark and cramped than the cabinet would be," I pointed out. "The recess created by the back of the window seat will allow for a secure perch. I'll take you there later and show you."

She sighed. "I certainly hope this works."

I heartily agreed. "Will you be all right by yourself for now? I have more arrangements to make."

Cassie waved a dismissive hand. "I plan to spend most of the day in the sunroom with a book, away from the gossips. It doesn't seem likely that anyone will be out-of-doors today." She inclined her head toward the windows, just now splattered with the first raindrops.

"If you really want to put the cats in a twist, you and Mr. Kendall can play checkers when he comes down." I winked.

Cassie laughed, startling the aforementioned tabbies, who swiveled their heads in our direction. "That's not a bad idea."

After inquiring of the cook's assistant—the kitchen staff knows everything that goes on—I found Josh Taggart in the stables with his son, cleaning saddles and harnesses. The beagle dozed on a hay bale in the corner.

Lucas sprung to his feet, dropping his cleaning rag. "Hullo, miss. You didn' want to go riding today, did you? The rain's only gonna get worse."

I shook my head. "I'm sorry to disturb your work."

"Not at all." Taggart gestured with his brush. "We're taking advantage of the weather to get a bit of cleaning done." He gave his son a pointed look. "Those harness buckles ain't gonna shine themselves."

The boy picked up his rag and resumed rubbing.

"I'm not interested in a ride, but I do need a favor." I gestured over my shoulder.

Taggart followed me outside, to the overhang that sheltered us from the rain but kept us out of earshot of the child. Taggart's brow furrowed as I explained what we had found last night.

"The moonshine doesn't surprise me, and Lucas told me he found a tunnel awhile back, but a body…." He shook his head in disbelief. "What is it you want me to do?"

"I need you and Mr. Kendall to wait in the underground room tonight. He'll unlock the door. Between the two of you, I think you can manage whoever comes along."

Taggart raised a skeptical brow. "You mean, the murderer? After all these years? How do you know he'll come?"

"I will do my best to…motivate him." *If* the guilty one was actually here tonight. It was a leap of faith. Or desperation.

"You can count on me, miss."

"Thank you." I nodded toward the boy, blond head bent over his task. "I'm also grateful to Lucas. I never would have found the tunnel without him. He's an observant child."

Taggart nodded. "That he is. Sometimes it's hard, raising him alone with my wife gone, but I am lucky to have him at all. She had trouble bearing children, you see." A shadow crossed his face. "We have Doc Marsh to thank for the boy."

My abdomen clenched in remembrance of my own loss, years ago. Some things were not meant to be. "She died giving birth to Lucas?"

He shook his head. "After Lucas. She knew it was dangerous for her, but wanted to give me—" He broke off, clearing his throat in embarrassment.

"I should let you get back to your work," I said quickly. "Thank you for your help."

Kendall had come downstairs by the time I returned. He appeared well rested and in good spirits. He crossed the foyer as I shook the rain from my shawl. "The arrangements are made?" he murmured.

"Almost." I eyed the foyer windows. In the garden beyond, the wind and rain battered the rose bushes. If this kept up, there wouldn't be a petal left. "We can only hope the local guests can still attend." Everything depended upon that. If we had to postpone the séance, the smugglers might return in the meantime and come upon the disturbed grave. What if they removed the evidence? We would never find Artie Willis's body again.

The most prudent step, of course, would be to contact the authorities immediately, as Meyer had suggested. Why was I reluctant to do so? Perhaps it was pride. Even though my original assignment did not include discovering the whereabouts of Artie Willis and catching his murderer, how could I step away from the chance to do so?

Very well, I admit—it was pride.

If we did not have the séance tonight, I would have to swallow that pride and allow Meyer to contact the sheriff.

The sound of voices drew our attention to the Rose Room. Guests were gathering at the card tables. "What did you tell Miss Joubert when she discovered you this morning?" I asked.

Kendall grimaced. "If you heard that, then you heard all of it." He glanced through the open door, where Amalie Joubert was being helped into a chair by the attentive Spencer Rayburn. Over Rayburn's shoulder, she fixed Kendall with an icy stare.

He stifled a sigh.

"You care a great deal for the young lady," I observed.

"Do not try matchmaking, Madame. It won't work with *me*. Besides, I couldn't possibly marry." His lip curled. "It would not be amenable to my line of work and hardly fair to the young lady."

"Your 'line of work' is not a foregone conclusion," I retorted. "A man with your...skills...could do all sorts of useful things."

He folded his arms. "Are you trying to reform me? If I remember correctly, yesterday you had no wish to turn me into a 'model of good citizenship. '" He dropped his voice."I heard that Meyer has recovered the jewels. I notice you did not reveal my role. Thank you for that."

I gave a short nod and headed for the stairs. There seemed nothing more to say. Still, I held out hope for the man.

That evening our arrangements were in place. Cassie and I—both of us in our stockinged feet, so as to make no noise—had climbed down the concealed passage between her room and the dining room, leaving behind the bell, a lantern, and matches.

Just before dinner, she withdrew from the company, claiming a sick headache. I overheard Mrs. Barrington whisper to Miss Joubert that Cassie's malady was likely because she could not bear the company of "decent women." I gritted my teeth but said nothing.

After dinner, Kendall affected disinterest in all matters of the supernatural kind and made a show of retiring to his room to read.

Although the veracity of Granny's knee was indeed borne out, the thunderstorm did not deter the locals. I was gratified to see that Captain Traub had accepted the invitation, along with the other guests we were expecting—Judge Knox, Dr. Marsh, Mr. Atwater, and Mrs. Becham. We were quite a large group, as Rayburn, Miss Joubert, Meyer, Mrs. Davis, the Barringtons, and the Hollisters joined us.

I seated Atwater on my left and Traub on my right. Once everyone was in position, I extinguished all of the lights except for a single candle in the middle of the table, which illumined a small bell under a glass dome. The rumbles of thunder and flashes of lightning through the windows created an ideal backdrop. I would need all the help I could get.

The ladies shifted uneasily in the gloom.

"We are attempting to communicate with whatever spirit resides in this place," I intoned. "I will call upon my spirit guide, Lady Isabella, a fourteenth-century young noblewoman who died in the Plague. If she is willing, she can help us talk to the spirit of this inn, so we can learn what is keeping it here." I nodded toward Meyer. I could see in the flickering light that his face had grown pale, despite being aware of the pretense. "Depending upon what the ghost wants from us, we may be able to encourage it to move on."

"What is the bell for?" Miss Joubert asked.

"My guide rarely speaks, but she can respond to yes or no questions by ringing the bell." I hoped the sounds of the storm weren't interfering with Cassie hearing me through the wall.

"Now then," I continued, "let us begin by holding hands. We must create a circle of energy by which to draw the spirits to us." I clasped the dry, chapped hand of Traub and the clammy one of Atwater. "Please remain absolutely quiet, no matter what you may see or hear."

Recalling the procedure I'd practiced with Madame Violette, I closed my eyes and began to hum as if in a trance, swaying slightly back and forth. The only other sounds in the room were the rain lashing the windowpanes and the claps of thunder, which grew louder and more frequent. We would soon be in the very midst of the storm.

I stiffened, opening my eyes. "My lady? Are you here? Ring once for yes."

To my great relief, a muffled ring sounded. Dr. Marsh, startled, craned his neck toward the bell under the glass dome, which had not moved.

"Ah, my lady, we need your assistance. We must speak with the ghost that haunts this inn. Can you help us?"

Another ring. Traub's hand reflexively clasped mine more tightly. Atwater's was slippery with perspiration.

Suddenly, I closed my eyes and slumped in the chair. I heard a smothered exclamation from the head of the table, which was quickly *shush*ed.

I let out a deep groan and deepened my voice. "*Murder.*" I heard the rustle of fabric as people shifted in their chairs. "*Injustice!*"

Meyer cleared his throat. "May I ask a question of the spirit?"

The bell rang. He continued. "Who are you?"

"*Willis,*" I grunted out.

Sharp exclamations. I cracked one eye open. Mrs. Becham and Dr. Marsh leaned toward each other, mouthing words I could not hear.

"You were murdered?" Meyer asked. "Everyone thought you ran off to avoid debt."

"*They were wrong,*" I intoned.

"Wh-what do-do you want of us?" It was Mrs. Davis's voice, shaking with fear.

"*Someone disturbed my bones. Lay me to rest. Find my killer.*"

"Who killed you?" Judge Knox asked.

As if on cue—I could not have orchestrated it better—a bright flash of lightning filled the window, followed closely by a thunderclap so loud it shook the table and drowned out the sound of Cassie's rapping to end the session. Undoubtedly, a tree nearby had been struck. Everyone jumped. Traub and Atwater pulled their hands away.

I roused myself, rubbing my temples and assuming a disoriented air.

Mrs. Becham, ever the mother hen, came over and put her arms around my shoulders while Meyer lit the lamps. "Are you all right, dear? Here, have some water." She reached for the pitcher.

I clasped the tumbler in shaking hands and took a few sips. "Wh-what happened?"

Mrs. Becham frowned. "You don't know?"

I let out a breath. "When a spirit speaks through me, I have no awareness of what transpires. Were we successful? Did someone from the other side communicate with us?"

"Indeed, yes," the young Hollister girl spoke up with enthusiasm, ignoring her mama's warning frown. "It was a man, and he said he'd been *murdered*."

"That will be quite enough, young lady," Mrs. Hollister said sharply. "It is time for you to be in bed. I do not know what I was thinking, allowing you to participate in such nonsense."

This seemed to be the general cue for both families to send the youngsters back to their rooms. Once they had gone, Meyer stood. "This is a worrying turn of events. Could Artie Willis have been murdered and his body buried somewhere on the property?"

I hid a smirk behind my handkerchief. Meyer was playing his part perfectly.

"Impossible," Judge Knox said. "I remember when he disappeared. There was a thorough search made. They found nothing."

Of course, the searchers hadn't known about the tunnel and the rooms below the inn.

Dr. Marsh got up and smoothed his trousers. "I agree. It is useless to speculate." He turned to his host and then to me. "It's time I should be going. Thank you for an interesting evening, Madame." He bowed.

"I'll ride with you," Judge Knox said.

Meyer glanced out the window. "You may want to wait a bit. It looks bad out there."

As everyone got up to look out the window, Lucas ran in. His pale hair was plastered to his head—except for one stubborn cowlick sticking up in back—and his wet clothes clung to him.

Mrs. Davis clucked her tongue. "Child, you are dripping water all over my clean floor."

Lucas was hopping up and down with excitement. "Mr. Meyer, sir—the big oak came down across the gate. We can't move it."

"What? Show me." With hurried apologies, Meyer followed the boy out, Dr. Marsh and Judge Knox close behind.

The rest of us retired to the Rose Room to wait. They returned twenty minutes later, dripping and exhausted.

"Here, Lucas, come closer to the fire." Mrs. Davis wrapped an afghan around the shivering boy and guided him to a seat. She turned to Meyer. "I'll fetch towels and hot coffee."

"And have rooms prepared," Meyer called after her. He passed a weary hand over his damp scalp. "We're going to need help tomorrow to cut our way out. We're trapped for tonight."

Amid the general hubbub, I excused myself to retire.

Cassie was waiting in her room, her impatience barely restrained. "Well? Do you know who it is? Did the guilty one give himself away?"

I shook my head. "I hadn't really been expecting that. But I'm hopeful he will reveal himself tonight. If I were to make a guess, I would say it is either Traub or Atwater who killed Willis. They could have planned it together. They would then have been free to take over the moonshine operation once the search for Willis had been given up."

Cassie clasped her hands in her lap. "Pen, it seems terribly dangerous to wait down there for the killer to appear. What if he's desperate?"

"Mr. Kendall is already there, as is Mr. Taggart."

"No, not Taggart. I saw him from my window. He ran over to where the oak came down."

Drat, I'd forgotten. "Perhaps Taggart will rejoin us when he's able." I crossed to the window and looked out. Lightning still flashed across the sky, and the rain was coming down in torrents. "Our killer may not brave such weather." I hated to think this was all for naught. I pushed open the panel to the secret passage.

"I'll come with you," Cassie said.

I sighed. Sometimes her courage came at inconvenient times. "I cannot risk your safety."

"But I want to help."

"You have already been of tremendous help."

"I can at least keep the panel open and listen," Cassie persisted. "If I hear you call for help, I'll get Mr. Meyer or Mr. Rayburn."

I grimaced. Meyer couldn't possibly fit into the space. "All right, but you had better fetch Mr. Rayburn if it comes to that." He was more a man of action anyway. "And please, do *not* come down the passageway unless I call."

"I promise." Cassie nodded. "Good luck."

CHAPTER 21

J climbed down the crawl space. When I reached the trap door at the bottom, I knocked softly. It was pulled open from the other side. There stood Phillip Kendall, reassuringly solid in the lamp light.

"Ah, Madame, you are just in time." He helped me down, his hands lingering at my waist a shade longer than necessary. "By the way, what is your real name?"

I was grateful for the dim light that hid my flushed cheeks. "Penelope Hamilton."

He clasped my hand and bowed over it. "A pleasure to meet you at last, Miss Hamilton."

I pulled away. "If you please, Mr. Kendall, this is not an assignation. We are here to catch a murderer."

He held up his hands in mock surrender. "As you wish. The séance was successful?"

I nodded. "If the killer was among the company, he is sufficiently anxious by now. He will want to check the grave. Is Taggart coming back?"

Kendall shook his head. "We could feel the tree crash, even

from down here. I knew he had to see to it. I told him not to return. We don't want him to inadvertently spring the trap."

I could see his point, but I felt uneasy. There were only two of us now. What if the killer brought a weapon? I listened to the rain and the wind, battering the sides of the structure above us. "We had better extinguish the lantern now. In this storm, we won't hear anyone approach until it's too late. He would see the light."

So we waited, he behind the door and me crouched in the far corner with the dark lantern, matches in hand. The blackness was total.

It was difficult to tell how much time elapsed. I may have dozed. A slight rustle jerked me to my senses. There was a glow beneath the door now. At the sound of a voice, I held my breath and strained to listen.

"Hold the light closer." It was a woman. I recognized her voice. *Mrs. Davis.* How could that be?

A male voice murmured something in reply.

My heart pounded. *Two.* We still had the advantage of surprise, but would that be enough? I set down the matches and joined Kendall beside the door. He grasped my hand briefly in encouragement. We were as ready as we could be.

The door swung wide, nearly to our faces, and light flooded the room.

"Over there, if I remember," the man said.

Kendall and I exchanged a glance. *Dr. Marsh.* Why would a kindly country doctor murder the innkeeper? How did he know about the tunnel? Was he a moonshiner as well? Why would the housekeeper help him?

They were moving toward the pallet that covered the shallow grave, in the far corner of the chamber. Kendall motioned me back, crept toward the pair, and launched himself at them. As the three of them fell, the doctor's lantern flew out of his hand and broke upon the pallets, plunging us in darkness.

I called out as I groped for my own lantern and matches. "Stop! It's over." The sounds of struggle went on.

By the time I had the lantern lit and pointed toward them, Kendall had Marsh pinned. He had difficulty keeping him subdued, however, as Mrs. Davis clutched at Kendall's arm. "Let him go!"

"Mrs. Davis, stop!" I called again.

She whipped around, eyes wide. "*You!* What is the meaning of this?"

I gestured to the back wall. "Sit down. Over there."

Kendall huffed to catch his breath as he helped Marsh to his feet. "You too, doctor."

Marsh fixed us in a glare before ineffectually brushing off his damp trousers and sitting beside the housekeeper.

I looked at Kendall. His hair was standing on end, one shirt-sleeve was ripped at the elbow, and a bruise bloomed along his forehead. "Are you all right?"

He nodded.

I turned to the pair. "Now then, what are you two doing here?"

Mrs. Davis opened her mouth to speak, but Marsh put a hand on her arm. "None of your business, Madame. Or should I call you *Mrs. Wynch?*"

Kendall gave me a startled glance. "Wynch? How many names do you have?"

I waved an impatient hand. "I'll explain later." How had the doctor known? Then I remembered. "The telegram at the stage-coach depot. You must have heard me being paged."

Marsh nodded. "I knew you were not who you claimed. I've had my eye on you ever since."

His eye on me.... "You saw me come out of the tunnel, the day of the fishing party. Is that when you told Mrs. Davis to search my room?"

A soft inhalation from the lady told me I was right.

I pointed at the pallet that covered the grave. Kendall pulled it away. "Did you fear I would discover Willis's body?"

Marsh's shaggy eyebrows nearly met his hairline. He exhaled a ragged breath. "How did you know?"

"We found it quite by accident. I staged the séance to lure you here. I must admit, I did not expect the two of you."

Marsh cleared his throat. "I am the one responsible for Artie's death. Hannah has nothing to do—"

"No," the housekeeper interrupted quietly. She met his eyes, as if they were the only two in the room. "You have protected me long enough. I am grateful. I won't allow you to take the blame."

Kendall sucked in a sharp breath. "Mrs. Davis, *you* killed Willis?"

She swallowed. "It-it was an accident. I only wanted him to stop—" She began to sob on Marsh's shoulder.

I realized my mouth had dropped open. My theory was in tatters. I took a breath. "What happened?"

Dr. Marsh put a protective arm around the housekeeper. "Hannah worked for me at the time, assisting in my dispensary. I sent her to Willis's place to buy brandy before he left town for the season."

"You would buy from a moonshiner, doctor?" Kendall asked.

The man shrugged. "Ten years ago, Bittern Point was far off the beaten path. Supplies weren't easy to come by, or cheap. Willis had a ready stock of rum and brandy. Although I wouldn't touch his rum, his brandy was of fair quality and has medicinal uses." He glanced at Mrs. Davis. "Naturally, when I sent her on the errand, I had no idea he would—well, he lured her to this isolated spot on the pretense of retrieving a bottle from his supply."

The woman was shivering uncontrollably. I bent down and put my shawl over her shoulders. "Mrs. Davis, did Willis...force himself upon you?" I asked, gently.

She gave a mute nod and hid her face in the shawl.

"Zeke brought her to me...afterward," Marsh said. "She was

hysterical. I treated her injuries and then came to see what could be done for Willis. I found him here, Hannah's scissors still in his chest. He was past all hope."

"So you buried the body," I said. "Why? It was self-defense. She could have explained what happened."

He shook his head. "She was in an extremely fragile state. She would not have withstood the sheriff's questions or, Heaven forbid, a public trial. I sent her to a sanitarium to rest. Zeke agreed to stay quiet. He had no love for Willis."

"But why bury him here? Why not drop the body in the lake?"

Kendall winced. I've been told that my frank way of speaking can be disconcerting.

"It was winter," the doctor said. "The lake was frozen. Everything shuts down around here. There seemed little risk of discovery. Zeke checked the house, found that the staff had already left and Willis was packed. I disposed of his bag. No one missed him until the spring, when he failed to re-open the inn. The Chestertown sheriff didn't know about the tunnel or these rooms Willis had constructed."

"But after his death, others took over the moonshine business," Kendall interrupted. "Former associates who knew about the tunnel. Didn't you worry about them finding the body?"

Marsh sighed. "I made sure to go...deep. I don't know how you managed to find it. But if Atwater or Traub *had* found the body, they wouldn't be likely to call attention to the fact. It would ruin their entire operation."

Kendall leaned forward. "So it *is* Atwater and Traub who are running things now."

Marsh waved a dismissive hand. "People talk. In a small place like this, there are few secrets." He sighed. "Now there are even fewer."

"But Meyer does not know?" I asked.

Marsh shook his head. "He hasn't been here that long."

"Why didn't Atwater or Traub buy the place outright, so they could continue making moonshine uninterrupted?" I asked.

Marsh grimaced. "The way I heard it, they would have. But renovations to Cedar Lodge overextended Atwater, and Traub never seems to have money. I have no idea what he does with it. Once Meyer moved in, they tried to undercut his business and drive him out."

Kendall pulled out a clean handkerchief and crouched down to hand it to Mrs. Davis, whose sobs had subsided to sniffles. "Why did you come back to Schroon Lake Inn when it holds such ugly memories for you?"

The lady wiped her eyes. "It was because of Jacob. For years, I'd kept house for him in the city. It had always been a dream of his to run a country inn. He knew I'd grown up around here, so he searched the area for a suitable place. I love him. I would have followed him anywhere."

"So he doesn't know?"

She shook her head. "I would rather...die...than tell him."

Phillip Kendall's expression softened in sympathy as he met my glance. He knew the difficult choice I had to make.

When I first became a detective, I thought it was for the money, the independence, the adventure. But I've come to realize there is more. Discovering the truth. Seeing justice done. Sounds lofty, I know, but there it is.

Here, however, the line between victim and wrongdoer was hopelessly blurred.

My pride was being sorely tested in this case. I'd been hired to expose the secrets of Schroon Lake Inn. But doing so could cause further harm.

I took a breath. Some things are more important than pride. I had already suppressed one truth. Heaven help me, I hoped Mr. Pinkerton would approve my decisions when he read my report.

Everyone looked at me expectantly. I squared my shoulders. "We shall have Mr. Meyer send for the sheriff as soon as the tree has been cleared. Mr. Kendall and I will show him the bones and the signs of recent moonshine activity. He can draw his own conclusions."

Marsh flashed me a grateful look as he helped Mrs. Davis to her feet.

Kendall grinned. "Let's get out of here."

CHAPTER 22

Taggart and Lucas, the beagle shadowing their steps, carried our luggage out to the waiting coach. Cassie and I lingered in the foyer to say goodbye to Hannah Davis and Jacob Meyer. The latter gave me a hearty handshake. "I will be writing William with a glowing review." He winked. "Even though you didn't catch the murderer."

I suppressed a sigh. "Thank you, sir." Perhaps Mrs. Davis would tell him the truth one day.

As expected, the Chestertown sheriff had thrown up his hands at the thought of another investigation after all these years. With the remains of Artie Willis on their way to a proper burial and the tunnel sealed off by the federal revenue men, Schroon Lake Inn would no longer be haunted by its past. The authorities were questioning Atwater and Traub even now and searching for the current location of the illegal distillery. Those two were looking at a heap of trouble.

I turned to Hannah Davis. "Best of luck to you both."

She clasped my hands and gave me a rare smile. It had a bit of a lopsided quirk to it that dimpled one cheek and made her look

ten years younger. The effect was startling. "We are grateful, miss."
With an awkward bob, she hurried to the kitchen.

Cassie touched my sleeve. "Ready?"

"Almost. You go on ahead. I'll catch up in a couple of minutes."

She frowned as she checked her watch. "Don't be long. The
coach is leaving soon."

The other guests had left the day before, except for Phillip
Kendall. I found him in the rose garden. "I thought you would
come to say goodbye."

He grimaced. "I am not very good at goodbyes."

"What are your plans after this?" I hoped they involved a
certain young lady, although Miss Joubert's coldness in the days
preceding her departure indicated otherwise.

He thrust his hands in his pockets and kicked at a pebble in the
dirt. "My original plan—Lady Montgomery's end-of-summer ball
—lacks the appeal it used to."

I chuckled. "Creeping through dark tunnels to catch
lawbreakers is much more fun. Admittedly, it spoils one for other
pursuits, such as lifting jewels from pretentious necks." I
suspected he was tired of being on the wrong side of the law for
so long.

He barely met my eye. "My days of 'pretentious necks' are at an
end. I think you already knew that." He took a breath. "What will
you put in your report to Mr. Pinkerton? Should I expect the law
to come knocking upon my door?"

I bit my lip. "I am duty-bound to make a full report to my
employer. However, I will emphasize certain mitigating circum-
stances. You returned the jewels, you assisted me in discovering
both the moonshine operation and Willis's body, and you
protected Miss Leigh and me, at great risk to yourself, from those
men in the tunnel."

"You think that will be enough? Is he not obligated to turn me
in to the authorities?"

"I'm confident that he will be grateful for your aid. Remember, the agency is not an arm of the law, unless specifically deputized to act in that capacity. My assignment was to resolve the hauntings at the inn and prevent further thefts. I have done that, and more. All are satisfied." Except for Atwater and Traub, of course. I smiled to myself.

Kendall's face brightened. "Please convey my thanks to Mr. Pinkerton and my heartfelt offer to assist either of you in the future. Whatever you may need." He dug into his pocket and handed me his card. "You can always reach me at this address."

I smiled as I tucked it in my reticule. What an interesting idea. Although most of the agents I knew were of impeccable background, occasionally there were, shall we say, *irregular* hires. Kendall may have volunteered for more than he realized.

He took my gloved hand in his. "Thank you, Miss Hamilton. May I call you Penelope?"

I shook my head. "I prefer Pen. And you may do so on one condition."

"Oh? What is that?"

"You straighten out your misunderstanding with Miss Joubert. You never told her the truth, did you?"

Kendall spread his hands in mock exasperation. "You still have not given up reforming me. I'm already turning away from a life of crime, aren't I? One drastic transformation at a time will suffice."

I left him to his solitude and headed for the pavilion, where our coach waited, Lucas standing beside it.

"They're ready to leave, miss," he said. "Shall I help you aboard?"

I smiled. "Thank you, young man." I pressed one last coin into his palm as he handed me up.

Cassie slid over to make room. "Quite an adventure! I will miss the beauty of this place, but it will be good to get home."

I looked back as we pulled away. The boy waved. Bright

141

sunlight reflected the white blond of his tousled hair and his crooked grin.

I started. The similarity to a certain housekeeper—the pale hair, the stubborn cowlick, and the warm, lopsided smile I had seen for the first time today—was unmistakable.

I sent her to a sanitarium to rest, Marsh had said.

How long had Mrs. Davis stayed there? Long enough, obviously. Had the doctor then arranged for the childless Taggarts to adopt Lucas?

We have Doc Marsh to thank for the boy, Josh Taggart had said. I thought he had meant something else entirely.

I kept my eye on Lucas was we cleared the drive. Mrs. Davis knew, I was sure of it. I had seen her tenderness toward the child. Jacob Meyer wasn't the only reason she had braved the bitter memories and returned here.

There are few secrets in a small place like this, Dr. Marsh had said. *Now there are even fewer.*

I settled back against the cushions with a sigh. There was still one secret at Schroon Lake Inn. And I was committed to keeping it.

∼

THE END

AFTERWORD

I hope you enjoyed the novella! Please consider leaving a quick review at your favorite online venue. A single sentence as to whether or not you liked it, along with clicking on the star rating you see fit, can go a long way! Ratings create a digital "word of mouth" that help readers find books they will love, particularly those written by independently published authors. Thank you!

Don't miss any of k.b.'s releases! Sign up here, or go to:
kbowenmysteries.com/subscribe

MYSTERIES SET IN LATE-19TH CENTURY HARTFORD, CT

THE CONCORDIA WELLS MYSTERIES

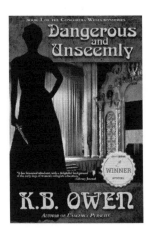

Set in a fictitious 1890s women's college, the series features Miss Concordia Wells, a young lady professor who cannot seem to resist a little unseemly sleuthing when those she cares about are at risk. Who knew higher education could be...murder?

Start with:

*Dangerous and Unseemly, book 1. Winner of **Library Journal's** "Best Mystery of 2015: SELF-e"!*

"A fun historical whodunit with a delightful background of the early days of women's collegiate education." ~*Library Journal*

ALSO BY K.B. OWEN

Dangerous and Unseemly, book 1 of the Concordia Wells Mysteries

Unseemly Pursuits, book 2 of the Concordia Wells Mysteries

Unseemly Ambition, book 3 of the Concordia Wells Mysteries

Unseemly Haste, book 4 of the Concordia Wells Mysteries

Beloved and Unseemly, book 5 of the Concordia Wells Mysteries

Unseemly Honeymoon, book 6 of the Concordia Wells Mysteries

Never Sleep, Chronicles of a Lady Detective, #1

The Case of the Runaway Girl, Chronicles of a Lady Detective, #3

ABOUT THE AUTHOR

K.B. Owen taught literature and writing for nearly two decades at universities in Connecticut and Washington, DC, and holds a doctorate in 19th century British literature. She has been a mystery lover ever since she can remember. Nowadays, she merges her love of detective fiction with her fascination for the Victorian era to create two series set in the late nineteenth-century United States: the *Chronicles of a Lady Detective* novella series and the Professor Concordia Wells Mystery novels.

K.B. is currently writing the seventh book in the Concordia Wells series, with an expected release date of February 2019.

Contact:
kbowenmysteries.com
contact@kbowenmysteries.com

facebook.com/kbowenwriter2

twitter.com/kbowenwriter

The Mystery of Schroon Lake Inn
the Chronicle of a Lady Detective

Cover design by Melinda VanLone, BookCoverCorner.com

ISBN-13: 978-0-9974674-9-9